WIGHT KNIGHT

Maureen Collins

Best Wishes

Maureen Collins

PUBLISHERS.

ISSBN 0 9539508 0 8

Maureen Collins has lived on the Isle of Wight for almost thirty years, her love of books was enhanced and encouraged by her English teacher, Doris Danby, who was Charles Dickens great granddaughter and Monica Dickens sister. As well as writing short stories and novels she is also an accomplished artist working in oils and watercolours.

'My love and thanks to my longsuffering husband, Bill. My mother, mother in law, and sisters for their hours of proof reading and especially my daughter in law, Angela, for her encouragement. Also my son Steven, for his help in preparing this story for publication. Grateful thanks to Gay Baldwin for her advice, and my vet Mr Jackson for his help with medical issues. But above all my praise to God for his gifts of love and creation.'

"Set me like a seal on your heart, like a seal on your arm.
For love is strong as Death, jealousy relentless as Hell.
The flash of it is a flash of fire, a flame of God himself.
Love no flood can quench, no torrents drown.
Were a man to offer all the wealth of his house to buy love,
contempt is all he would purchase."
Song of Songs.

1

The springs on the antique iron bed creaked when Kim sat up with a start. Her heart thumped wildly in her chest as she looked around the unfamiliar bedroom. For a second confusion swamped over her, and a frown pulled her elegantly arched brows together, as she listened intently for the noise that had disturbed her from her sleep. Suddenly, a gust of wind blew outside the window causing the overhanging branches of a large oak tree to scratch and patter menacingly against the rain streaked glass, sounding like some lost soul trying to find a way in. The curtain billowed out and rustled against the top of the old dressing table mirror adding to the ghostly sounds. Somewhere in the distance a clock chimed twice.

"Oh!" she gasped loudly jumping in surprise as a flash of lightning lit up the room, casting eerie shadows that took on all sorts of grotesque shapes. The door creaked open then shut suddenly with a loud bang.

"W-who's there?" she called out in fright, pulling the sheet up to her neck for protection and listening to the silence for an answer, hearing only the erratic beat of her heart thrumming in her ears. Fiona had told her a ghost haunted the place! For a moment she sat trembling, frozen with fear, her breathing laboured, until her logical mind took over. "For goodness sake, pull yourself together you stupid idiot, haunted indeed! It's a storm, that's all," she snapped irritably at her own nervousness as she realised the wind had caused the door to slam.

Letting go of the sheet that had temporarily given her protection, she pushed her long thick hair away from her face with trembling fingers then clicked on the bedside lamp, which immediately gave a reassuring glow. The springs of the bed moaned again in protest as she threw back the covers and swung her long legs out. Padding barefoot across the room to shut the window another flash of lightning illuminated the room and she counted until the thunder rumbled. "One, two, three, four five six...ten miles away," she informed the reflection of the classically beautiful woman staring back at her in the shiny glass, dressed in a sensible white broderie anglaise night-gown. She grinned at her image, if she'd seen that a moment ago she would have sworn she'd seen the ghost. Grunting with effort she pulled at the old sash window trying unsuccessfully to close it.

"What the...?" she leapt back in shocked consternation from the pane as a shower of small stones hit the glass.

"Kim!" an anxious voice stage whispered from the small front garden below. "Kim, please! Wake up, it's me Fiona!"

With all her strength Kim pushed at the window and managed to move it a few inches, just enough for her to stick her head out to look down at the pretty face of her twin sister.

Screwing up her face as the wind drove the rain into it, she answered, "Fiona! What are you doing out there? It's two o'clock in the morning and..."

"Will you let me in, I know what bloody time it is, hurry...I need your help!" Fiona cried obviously very distressed, turning urgently to look behind her.

"I'm on my way," Kim stated hurriedly, hearing the fear in her sibling's voice.

"Now what was Fiona playing at?" Kim mumbled, wiping the rain away from her face and drawing her full mouth into a straight line. Snatching up her dressing gown from the back of the door, which only moments ago had taken on the image of a tall man when the light of the storm had lit the room, she tied the sash irritably around her slender middle. "Couldn't my sister keep out of trouble for just one day?" she asked herself as she ran nimbly down the narrow staircase to the front door.

Anxiously throwing back the bolts and opening the heavy oak door, she gasped in surprise as a figure dressed totally in black from head to foot, lunged at her.

"Oh Kim, thank goodness you heard me!" Fiona practically fell into the hall gasping for breath, she was soaking wet from the rain and shivering with fright. "Quick," she whispered with breathless urgency, "shut the door!"

Kim's large sapphire blue eyes widened and looked apprehensively over Fiona's shoulder out into the dark night expecting to see the devil himself behind her sister. A flicker of blue light, followed close by a loud crackle of thunder urged her into action; she shut the wooden door with a resounding bang.

"Put the other bolt on!" Fiona demanded anxiously, bending down to the lower one.

"Here let me!" Kim tutted, pushing her sister's shaking fingers aside, finishing the job for her. "What on earth's going on? I thought you were asleep in the other room!"

"I-I went out to meet Alex," she replied with a sigh, pulling off the black knitted hat and lowering her head in shame, the soft honey coloured curls fell from the restraining clasp and covered her face.

"But...I thought...Fiona!" Kim cried out in consternation. "You asked me to come here to the Isle of Wight with you so that you could get away from him, why is he here? He's married for heaven's sake!"

Fiona lowered herself down on the bottom stair and buried her golden head in her hands and sobbed. "I-I'm so sorry, I-I can't help it...I love him and he loves me, I lied to you. I really came here to be nearer to him. His brother lives in the village, the big Manor House down the road belonged to his parents. Alex arranged to spend some time with him. We saw it as an opportunity to meet without his wife finding out, only she just has!"

"Fiona!" Kim exclaimed horrified.

"Please don't be cross," Fiona begged, "you don't know the full story, his wife doesn't..."

"Understand him!" Kim finished with a derogatory air, folding her arms across her chest.

"No, I was going to say his wife doesn't get on with his brother...she wasn't suppose to come with him. But she's here Kim, and she was waiting for me..." Fiona raised her lovely white, tear stained face and looked into her sister's eyes. "S-She just tried to kill m-me...she's absolutely mad!"

"Well I wouldn't be that pleased if my husband was meeting his lover either!" Kim chided brushing her long blue-black hair away from her beautiful face.

"No, I mean she's mentally ill," Fiona shuddered and started shaking uncontrollably, "she's always injuring Alex. Oh Kim, she had a gun!"

Kim stared cynically at her sister for a while trying to assess the situation, then seeing her shaking with trepidation, took pity. "Come on let's get you out of those wet clothes before you catch your death of cold."

Kim clicked her tongue as she helped Fiona to her feet and started taking off the black waterproof jacket, shaking the moisture off before hanging it on the hall-stand. "The fire's still glowing in the lounge, go and sit by it while I make you a cup of sweet tea, then we'll talk."

'Gun indeed!' Kim mused as she bustled her way down the narrow hall into the kitchen; 'First ghosts now guns, Fiona always made a drama out of everything!'

Kim put the tray down on the hearthrug and handed a mug of steaming liquid to a more composed Fiona. "Thanks, who would think you were the youngest, you always were the sensible one Kim, feet on the ground, you're just like Dad!"

"Supposing you start from the beginning," Kim invited ignoring the flattery, youngest indeed, only by ten minutes! "I might not feel so sensible after you've told me the whole story!" she grimaced as she reached over and flicked the table lamp on.

"Turn it off!" Fiona hollered jumping up from her seat, almost spilling her tea, her big brown eyes full of terror.

"Really!" Kim balked, but turned it off all the same as a tingle of fear ran like icy fingers down her spine. 'Goodness what's wrong with you? You never usually allow your imagination to run wild, it must be this old cottage, it has a strange atmosphere!' she shuddered and reprimanded herself. Irritably she turned to her sister, "Right now the light's off, are you going to tell me what's going on?"

Fiona sat down again, took an unsteady deep shuddering breath. "Trisha...Alex's wife, suffers from a mental disorder...she...she abuses Alex...hits him. Alex tried to cope with her violence, but after three years of hell he moved out of the marital home and started divorce proceedings. Now that she could no longer harm him she turned the tables by threatening to harm herself if he ever went through with the divorce."

"Surely she was only crying wolf?" Kim chipped in.

"I wish! We met three months after he left her. Trisha found out about us and took an overdose, she ended up in hospital. Alex blamed himself; he felt sort of responsible and went back to her on the condition she underwent medical help."

"But what about you?"

"We talked it over, we had only just met, I encouraged him to give his marriage another try."

"You never told me, it must have been very hard for you!"

"As I said we had only just met, I was falling for him but I wasn't sure how he felt about me."

Kim squeezed her sister's hand, "Trying to save the marriage obviously didn't work."

"For a while it seemed to be working, but within two months they were back to square one, she refused the help that was being offered and the abuse started again."
"I didn't realise, poor Alex!" Kim stated, tears forming in her compassionate eyes.
"Indeed," Fiona agreed glad that Kim was showing signs of softening a little. "On many occasions he would end up in A & E because of the physical attacks."
"Why did he put up with it, what sort of a man is he for allowing her to do it?"
Fiona pouted indignantly at her sister's criticism and came instantly to his defence, "He's a good man, and he put up with it because he was afraid she'd kill herself if he left. Anyway," she shrugged, "what man likes to admit he's being bullied by a woman?"
Kim nodded, "Not many I suppose, I'm sorry, go on..."
"Alex and I tried to stay away from one another but after the abuse started again we realised we had fallen in love...I...We really did try to end it," she sniffed again and flicked a tear away, "but it's impossible, he was so unhappy and we love one another so much. Until we can work out what is the best thing to do, we've decided to meet secretly, snatching a moment here and there."
"But I don't see why you had to meet him here?" Kim interrupted.
"I told you, Alex's family home is just outside the village, his father died last year and his older brother, Sebastion, needed him here to discuss his father's estate now that the will has gone through probate. It seemed like the perfect opportunity, Trisha refused to come with him because she dilikes his brother so much. Alex has come into half his father's estate so she was more than happy for him to come alone...she allows anything if money is involved," she mused bitterly. "We thought we had a whole fortnight together!"
"Using me as a smoke screen!"
"Yes and no, we can only meet at night, honest Kim, don't be cross, I really do need your company too..."
"Does his brother know you're here, is he part of this...this... deceit?"
"Goodness me no!" Fiona scowled at her sister's choice of words. "They're not very close, Alex could never confide in Seb. He's a miserable old tyrant with strong archaic views on what's right and what's wrong!"
"How do you mean?"
"He would consider our relationship as adulterous! Anyway Seb holds a grudge against Alex," she stated flippantly, pulling her mouth into a pout again.

"Why?"
"When Alex finished university he was supposed to go home and help run the estate, which, thanks to his father's excessive spending, was deeply in debt. There is a family title, which supposedly dates back to the Crusades, and his father liked to play the Lord of the Manor, he spent all the families' fortune, and started to sell off priceless paintings and works of art. When they were gone he re-mortgaged the property. The worry made his father very ill, that's when Seb gave up his chosen vocation to help his father, he expected poor Alex to do the same!" she mused indignantly.
"His chosen vocation?"
Fiona nodded, "He was in a monastery on the Island, Quarr Abbey, he was studying to become a monk."
Kim tutted, even though she was brought up a Catholic, she had never understood how anyone could deny themselves a normal life in order to show they loved God. What was it the Bible said, 'It is not good that man was alone; I will make him a helpmate...' pulling herself up from her self opinionated thoughts she asked, "so what happened?"
"I just told you, he came home, put his vocation on hold while he sorted out his father's…"
"No not that, what happened between them, why didn't Alex help his brother?"
"Alex didn't get on particularly well with his father, their mother kept the peace between them, but she died the same year, so he thought it was better to follow a different career!" she excused him.
"So Seb, the eldest brother, after giving up his vocation, was left with a family estate heavily in debt, to run on his own?" Kim finished for her.
Fiona nodded again, "It was for the best, Seb knew how to cope with his grieving father and the estate, he's a very clever business man, he was awarded a Knighthood."
"So he's a Sir as well as a Lord?"
"Yes, but he doesn't like anyone using either title, likes to be humble, anyway, Alex would only have caused them more misery if he'd come home," she continued.
Kim was beginning to feel deeply sorry for this older brother and thought Alex was beginning to sound rather selfish and weak, but who was she to make a judgement she reminded herself again. 'People are what they are, and nobody knew what was in their hearts when they made decisions!'
"Well that aside, tell me what happened tonight?"
Fiona sat hunched up on the armchair, both hands holding the steaming mug of sweet tea. "Alex and I arranged to meet by his brother's stables tonight. When you went to bed I waited until you were asleep, then I let

myself out of the back door and made my way to Ashill Manor, it's only across the field opposite," Fiona pointed to the front window. "Alex was supposed to be there. I was a little early and the storm came, the rain was so heavy I took shelter inside the stable. When the door opened, I thought it was Alex. I had the shock of my life when his wife came in! She was stood there aiming a gun at me!" She swallowed and shuddered as the memory came back. "Trisha threatened to k-kill me then t-turn the gun on herself. She told me she'd found an e-mail I'd sent to Alex on his home computer, confirming where I would meet him and what time, I don't think Alex knew she was on the Island, she didn't come with him, he was on the same ferry as we were."
"That was stupid of you to contact him at home! Are you sure she had a gun?" Kim questioned more than a little sceptical.
"I'm positive," she stated, her eyes glazed over as she recalled the events. "There was a noise outside the stable, I think it was Alex…it caught her off guard and she turned around…I-I took a chance and ran past her, she grabbed at my arm, after a bit of a struggle I managed to get away!"
"Thank God for that! Does she know you are staying here?"
"No."
"Well that's good, but I think we should inform the police, this is…"
"T-the police are p-probably already involved. A-as I left she fired a shot at me. It missed," she stated unnecessarily. Fiona took another trembling breath, "T-then…then I…I heard another shot, I think she either shot Alex or herself…" As if to confirm her words, the sound of sirens competed with the roar of thunder. "Oh Kim, that's an ambulance, he may be dead!" she wailed pressing her knuckles against her lips.
"You don't know that for sure, but I really think we should phone the police," Kim said comfortingly putting her arm around her.
Fiona broke down completely.
Waiting for the tears to subside Kim spoke, "Better now?"
"N-no," Fiona cried wringing a wet handkerchief unmercifully, "I-I wish I knew if Alex was alright."
"I'm sure he is, the noise that distracted his wife might not have been him, it could have been an animal or something," she suggested helpfully.

They both jumped when the telephone rang.
"That's got to be Alex, he's the only one who knows we are here," Fiona exclaimed with obvious relief, "he's alive!" She raced over to the big black telephone and picked the receiver up, "Alex are you alright?"
With a sob Fiona crumpled to the floor crying and laughing hysterically, "Oh thank God, oh Alex, I thought…I thought she'd shot you…we heard the ambulance."

Kim heard the man shouting at her down the line from where she was standing, "Fiona will you calm down and listen!"
Taking charge when she saw that her sister was in no state to hear him, she took the receiver from Fiona's unresisting hand.
"Alex? It's Kim here, Fiona's very upset can she phone you back?"
"No, listen I haven't got much time, I can't talk, Seb, my brother, has involved the police, Trisha is saying that she interrupted a horse thief who held a gun at her!"
"Oh dear," Kim muttered.
"It gets worse, she's claiming that the thief was armed but she managed to grab the weapon off her, and that it went off while they were wrestling!"
Kim's beautiful face drained of colour, she sat down heavily on the arm of the nearest chair. "But that's a lie, Fiona wouldn't do a thing like that, she wouldn't even know how to fire a gun, it wasn't her gun!"
"I know that! Somehow Trisha found out we were meeting at the stable...she made sure she got there before me, the gun belongs to Trisha and she injured herself when Fiona got away, I saw her do it!"
"So it was an ambulance siren, I-is she badly hurt?"
"No, just a flesh wound on her leg, Trisha never does too much damage to herself!" he grated sarcastically. "And the sirens you heard were from the police car. My brother, Seb, heard the shooting and arrived soon after, he saw Fiona running off."
"Oh dear!" she mumbled again.
"Don't worry he thought she was a youth! I heard the police say they suspected someone local. I think it's best that you keep silent over the incident and that I don't try to contact Fiona again until things have died down, is she alright?"
"Not really, and I disagree, I think Fiona should speak to the police..."
"Please don't do that!" he hissed urgently. "Trisha is a very...she want's revenge and she can be very convincing...please, at least wait until they have proved Fiona wasn't the owner of the gun..."
"I don't know, I always think honesty is the best policy..."
"Fiona could be wrongfully arrested for this, you wouldn't want to see her locked up in a cell overnight would you?"
Glancing quickly at her distraught sister, Kim worried the flesh on her bottom lip while she considered, "Alright," she agreed reluctantly, "but only until the ownership of the gun has been proved, but I'm not happy. However, I agree with your suggestion that you don't meet. We better stay on the Island for the duration, or else the police would become suspicious if we left now."
"I hadn't thought of that," he agreed. "Kim?"

"What?"
"I really love Fiona, I know things seem bad and that I look the biggest cad in town, but..."
"Just don't hurt her."
"That I can promise you, she's my soul mate! Look I have to go I'll be in touch..."
Kim stared down at the silent receiver for a while before she put it back into its cradle, then turning she tried to pacify the sobbing Fiona.

"Alright now?"
Fiona nodded and handed back the empty brandy glass. "Yes, I'm sorry I've caused you so much trouble."
Kim gave a small feminine snort, "I'm just glad nobody was badly hurt, I think we should try and get some sleep now, we'll talk more about it in the morning, the storm's past over in more ways than one!"

* * *

Groaning, Kim ran her hands through her thick hair as she descended the stairs. The shower had done nothing to clear her aching head, 'what a night' she pondered as she made her way into the small kitchen. Yawning, she filled the kettle and put it on the stove to boil. A few moments later Fiona walked into the kitchen. "Good morning," she uttered brightly as she took the orange juice out of the fridge and poured out a glassful, "want some?"
Kim nodded as she put the toast in the rack to cool. "We need to talk Fiona, if Alex's brother has involved the police and they think it's someone local, they are bound to do house to house enquiries. It would be helpful if we got our stories straight if we're not going to tell them the truth!" Kim added dolefully, she hated telling lies.
"No need, just tell them we went to bed at eleven, and don't look so concerned, it's not a lie, we did!" she smiled cheerfully, all the trauma of yesterday forgotten.
Kim frowned, 'strange how twins could be so different, Fiona was just like mother, brown-eyed dizzy blond, causing no end of chaos for herself and others, then bouncing back as it nothing had happened, while others were left to sort out the mess.'
"Why the frown?" Fiona asked putting the icy glass in her sister's hand.
"I have a headache, the storm didn't clear the air, I'm sure we're in for another, the sky looks really heavy," she commented truthfully, looking out of the window at the beautiful rolling West Wight countryside, effectively side stepping her sister's question. Her head really did hurt

and she was unwilling to get into an argument, she always ended up the loser anyway.
Fiona beamed back at her, "Yes, I was listening to the local radio earlier, the forecast says more to come, shall I get you some aspirins?"
"No thanks I'm sure a cup of tea will help." Kim raised her eyebrows and turned away from her sister's beautiful elfin face, to think that once she had envied her mother and her twin's fragile beauty! She smiled to herself as she poured out the tea, if Fiona was like Mum, then she was like Dad. Her smile broadened as she thought of the big Irish man, she loved him dearly. He was a big softie, unflappable, easygoing, anything for a quiet life, completely complimenting her mother's slightly zany personality. 'Even my colouring is the same as his,' she thought catching her classically beautiful features in the reflection of a mirror above the kitchen sink, her big blue eyes glanced sleepily back at her, the dark rings under them smudged her ivory complexion, bearing witness to the sleepless night. The only thing she had in common with Fiona was their build. Five foot four and slight, but, 'thank goodness,' Kim acknowledged 'that's where the likeness ended, totally non identical!'

The sisters had just finished washing the breakfast dishes when a sharp rap on the front door startled them both.
"I'll get it!" Fiona chirped breezily, throwing the tea towel down on the worktop, before she strolled nonchalantly down the hall to answer the door.
Kim stayed in the kitchen wiping the tops of the units, the tones of a deep male voice with a local accent, issued from the hall.
Fiona waltzed in, "It's a policeman!" she whispered dramatically. "Remember we both went to bed at eleven." Then raising her voice loud enough for the policeman to hear what she said, "It's the law Kim, he wants to speak to us, apparently some horse rustlers were in town!" she mimicked a western cowgirl. "He's asking if we heard or saw anything unusual last night!" she added brightly, raising her eyebrows.
Kim tutted disapprovingly as she took off her apron and hung it up, then dried her hands, before following her sister into the lounge, 'how could she act so blasé, didn't she realise how serious this situation was?'

A young policeman was standing looking out of the lounge window, turning his cap round and round in his hands. He turned and smiled when Kim and Fiona entered the room.
"Sorry to trouble you Miss, there's been an incident at Ashill Manor, that's the building over the other side of the field," he stated pointing towards the window. "We're doing house to house enquiries. Your

cottage is nearest, did you see or hear anything suspicious last night?"
"Sorry Officer I can't help you," Kim chose her words carefully trying not to lie, "I was disturbed by the storm but..."
"What time would that be?"
"It woke me around two..."
"Two o'clock you say, how do you know what time it woke you?" he interrupted tucking his cap under his arm and undoing the top pocket of his jacket to remove his note pad.
"I heard a clock chiming, I thought it chimed twice, I could be wrong...I got up to close the window, but..." she shrugged and looked apologetic.
"We went to bed around eleven, what time did all this happen?" Fiona took over.
"Early hours of the morning, Miss, it was around two, you said the storm woke you and you got up and shut the window, which window would that be Miss?" he enquired pencil poised.
"The one above this one," Kim mumbled cursing herself for saying she'd got up.
"Are you sure it was the storm that woke you?" he asked as he scribbled something down.
"Yes I'm absolutely sure, it was very noisy, could I offer you a cup of coffee?" she smiled sincerely attempting to change the subject.
"Thank you Miss but no," he smiled back, flipping the note pad shut and returning it to his pocket. "I have the rest of the village to interview, if you do see or hear anything suspicious, call the local station and don't worry I'm sure we'll catch him."
"I do hope so, it's a little worrying, are we safe here?" her twin sister added.
"I should think so, we think the thief was after Sir Seb Worsley's horses, there has been a spate of attempted stable thefts in the area, he couldn't have been after anything else, he didn't even bother breaking into the Manor House."
"Did he get any horses?" Fiona asked innocently as she led him towards the front door.
"No, Sir Worsley's sister-in-law interrupted him, poor lady was injured when she tried to wrestle a gun off him."
"Oh no, a gun! I-is she alright?"
"Luckily the bullet only grazed her leg, she didn't even need a stitch," he smiled reassuringly, putting his hat on as he went out the door. "Confused the poor woman though, she insisted the intruder was a woman!"
"A woman? Surely not?" Fiona questioned.
"I doubt it, Sir Worsley saw a youth running away, good day to you and

enjoy the rest of your holiday, remember if you notice anything amiss please contact us."
"We will, good day officer," Fiona smiled and fluttered her eyelashes coyly as she shut the door.
Kim muttered a silent oath as she listened to the conversation; Fiona was such an actress, no wonder her mother had wanted her to go to drama school instead of becoming an engineer.

"You were pushing your luck asking him all those leading questions," Kim scolded her sister when she returned to the lounge.
"Sorry, but I was trying to find out a little more."
"Well don't get too interested, the police might wonder why!" she warned quickly then changed the subject when she saw evidence of tears glistening in her sister's eyes, she couldn't cope with one of Fiona's tantrums, not today! "What shall we do today?"
"Don't know," Fiona replied sulkily.
"Then may I suggest we go sightseeing, Osborne House looks worth a visit, Prince Albert built it for Queen Victoria..."
"Sightseeing?"
"We are after all supposed to be tourists."
"Yes, I suppose so, Alex won't be able to get in touch with me today anyway," she added selfishly.
Sighing, Kim walked out of the room before she said something she would regret. Trust Fiona to think everything was fine now that it was out in the open!

2

"For pity's sake woman, all I'm asking you is what made you go out there on your own? It was a particularly stupid..."
"I've already told you, I couldn't sleep, the storm disturbed me, I looked outside the window, that was when I saw a dark figure slip into the stable," Trisha interrupted her brother-in-law, feeling angry that the surly scowling man was raising his voice at her. Knowing his horses were his pride and joy she cleverly changed her tactics. "I'm sorry Seb, I didn't stop to think for my own safety, I was so concerned, especially about Black Fury, he was making the most noise, so I went to investigate."
"You were extremely foolish, you should have woken me, don't you ever put your life at risk for an animal again, do I make myself clear?"
"Seb don't scold me. Anyway, how could I have gone to your bedroom? The last time I did, you misinterpreted my intentions, and I wasn't going to risk you thinking that of me again!" she complained sulkily, sitting herself up from a reclining position on the chaise lounge and wiping away an imaginary tear.
Unwilling to get into an argument about the 'misinterpreted incident' that had occurred shortly after her marriage, Seb turned away in disgust at the crocodile tears, muttering an expletive softly under his breath. He was very aware that everything Trisha did was a calculated act; concern for the horses indeed, the only thing she was concerned about was herself. He'd noticed that she didn't show any compassion towards Alex's injuries last night, which he said he'd received from getting in the way of the intruder and Trisha. Somehow he didn't believe him, something about the whole event didn't quite fit, a head injury like that would have knocked a man twice his size senseless!
Alex chose that moment to enter the lounge.

"Good morning, how are you feeling?" Seb asked, "Did you manage to get some sleep?"
Alex's hand touched the bruised lump on his forehead and cast a guarded glance at his wife. "Good morning, the tablets the doctor gave me sent me out like a light, I've a bit of headache but..."
"Oh for goodness sake don't make such a fuss Alex at least you weren't shot at! Some husband you are, don't bother asking how my poor leg is! Or thank me for saving our horses," Trisha purred sarcastically as she rubbed her bandaged leg, hoping it would get some sympathy.
Ignoring the woman's venom, Alex poured himself a coffee from a pot the maid had left on a trolley. "Have the police caught anyone?" Alex questioned his brother.
Seb frowned perplexed as he witnessed Trisha malicious spite towards her husband. Feeling more than a little angry with her, he ignored her outburst and answered Alex. "No the police haven't caught anyone yet, they think he was probably local or had a get-away car nearby..."
"He?" she turned on Seb. "How many times do I have to keep telling you, it was a woman!" Trisha hissed irately her temper flaring up from nowhere.
Seb eyes narrowed as he stared at her, 'the woman is not in her right mind,' he assessed. As if to confirm his thoughts she started to laugh. Then whispering under her breath, loud enough for Alex to hear she ranted on, "not just a woman either, was she Alex, it was your latest mistress, Fiona, and you know it!"
The two brothers exchanged a quick look. Alex looked slightly embarrassed, had Seb heard? If he had his expression gave nothing away.
"As I was saying," Seb skirted around the overheard accusation and ignored Trisha's maniacal outburst. "If he had a car he would have been miles away before the police even got here. He was probably just seeing how many horses I have." Seb emphasised the I, if this crazy woman thought his horses were part of their father's estate, then she could think again! "I expect he was a little disappointed when he discovered that the only horse worth taking was Black Fury. Nevertheless, I'll have to tighten security, I'm thinking of getting another dog while Susie is indisposed," he said tickling the ears of his very pregnant Rottweiler, "by the way who locked her up in the...?"
He stopped speaking as the butler opened the door and gave a polite cough to attract his attention. "Excuse me Sir, sorry to interrupt, but police inspector Marchent and a policewoman have arrived, shall I show them in?"
"No James, show them into my study, I'll speak to them in there," he ordered watching his brother and sister-in-law's faces intently, he

perceived his instincts were right, they knew more about this than they were both letting on. He would speak to Alex later.

"Good morning, sit down," Seb invited the inspector as he entered his office and shut the door firmly behind him. By the embarrassed look on the man's face, Seb had a feeling he wasn't going to like what the detective had to say.

The man gave a nervous cough and sat down. "Good morning, thank you Sir. Well Sir, um... we have made inquiries as to the ownership of the gun," he ran an embarrassed finger along the inside of the collar on his pristine white shirt, and sent his colleague a look before he continued. "We regret to have to tell you the gun was registered in the name of a Mrs Patricia Worsley, Sir. It seems she purchased it from a gun shop in Surrey a year ago." The man stopped and waited for the information to sink in.

"So the gun belongs to my sister-in-law?"

"Yes, I'm sorry Sir."

"Don't be, I suspected as much," Seb stated flatly, his face an angry mask as he started to put two and two together. "I'm sorry we've wasted your time inspector, Mrs Worsley is not enjoying the best of health. I suspect she took the gun to the stable with her because she saw the intruder. Fear probably made her disown the weapon, but she wasn't lying about an intruder, Inspector Marchent, I saw him running away. I believe by his stature and the way he was dressed that the intruder wasn't a thief but one of the young people who came to see the farm zoo last week, he was only a lad, knee-high to a grasshopper, I doubt he'd have harmed anyone."

The police inspector stood up, "Well we'll still keep a watchful eye on the place and we will of course have to confiscate Mrs Worsley's gun, perhaps the youth did us all a favour. At least it came to light that she owned a gun and a woman in her state of mind, well..." He didn't finish the sentence off.

"Quite," Seb agreed shuddering as he thought of the possible consequences. "What will happen to her?"

The inspector shrugged, "We have to arrest her and there may be a charge of threatening someone with a firearm, which, as you probably know, is a very serious offence. The fact that the young lad is unlikely to come forward with a complaint is in her favour, and I don't suppose he'll take the risk of coming back!"

Seb nodded grimly and stood up next to the older man. "Again I can only apologise that my family have wasted so much of your time."

"That's alright Sir, we will still continue with our house to house enquiries, two stables on a farm just outside Ventnor have been broken into this week, we thought this was another attempt by the same gang. I

don't know what they hope to achieve if they do manage to steal any horses, it would be nigh on impossible to take them off the Island unnoticed. One good thing to come out of all this incident, is that it has stepped up our inquiries, so we'll say no more about it."
"Thank you," Seb muttered shaking the inspector's hand. "Will you see Mrs. Worsley now?"
"Yes, We need a statement. I've brought WPC Holst with me for that reason."
Seb went to the door, "I'll get Mr and Mrs Worsley for you."

* * *

"Oh no!" Fiona cried, frantically shaking the black jacket she had worn last night around in the small hall. "Oh no!"
"What's wrong now?" Kim asked as she came down the stairs. "Are you ready? I thought we would have lunch out..."
"I've lost it!"
"Fiona calm down, lost what?" she asked watching her twin pull the sleeves of the jacket she was holding, inside out.
"The bracelet that Alex gave me," she whispered gloomily.
"Perhaps it's up in your room."
"I've searched everywhere," she cried.
"Are you sure you bought it with you?"
"Kim you don't understand, I was wearing it last night, when Trisha caught my arm, I felt something...I dropped it in the stable!"
"I'm sorry, perhaps Alex will find it or buy you a new one!"
"It was a family heirloom it belonged to his mother, Alex had my name engraved on it," she said flatly. "If it's found by the police, they will know I was there last night!"
Kim sank down on the bottom stair, "Oh Fiona!"
"What are we going to do?" Fiona asked forlornly.

* * *

Screwing her blackened face up against the pounding rain she glanced at the large grey stone thirtieth century Manor House. House? It was more like a small castle! An icy feeling ran down her spine causing her to shudder. Close up it was spooky and forbidding, why it even had towers! Did the owner keep maidens locked up in them? The thought of a medieval woman calling for help as she let down her long silken tresses from one of the slit windows made her smile. Gosh her imagination was working overtime! Pulling herself together, she concentrated on the task ahead. There were still lights on in the upstairs rooms; she would wait until they went out before making her way to the stables. The storm that had been threatening all day was approaching fast and if it was possible, it had begun to rain even heavier, shivering more from apprehension than cold, she pulled Fiona's black woollen hat down lower over her face. A crash of thunder followed close after the searing flash flickered across the stormy sky, causing an owl to hoot in terror as it fled for shelter into the tall trees. Startled Kim sucked in her breath stifling a scream, "boy what a backdrop!" she muttered under her breath, she could well believe the Island was the most haunted place in Britain!

Keeping well out of sight, Kim's face wore a sardonic expression as the last light went out. 'This is it, go for it kid, it's now or never,' she encouraged herself as she hurried silently towards the stable, keeping close to the trees and tying not to step into the deep puddles that were fast forming on the squelchy soil beneath her feet. 'What are we going to do indeed!' she mused as she remembered her sister's words. 'Please God let the stable door be open!' she prayed as she approached the building. She forced herself to reach for the doorknob. Even though her fingers were stiff and wet she managed to turn it. Amazingly it was open! Slipping in she closed it quickly behind her. With rasping breath that stung her dry throat, she shut her eyes and leant against the wooden door for a moment trying to still her jaded nerves and her rapid heartbeat. 'How come she always had the job of putting her twin sister's sins to right?'
"Where's the plan?" she asked herself patting her cold wet hands against the pockets of her sister's black jacket, searching for the piece of paper. Fiona had drawn her a diagram of the inside of the stable at least it would give her some idea of where to start looking. One of the horses snorted an answer, "Its alright I've found it!" she whispered reassurance to the animal, thankful that her job as a small animal vet sometimes brought her into close contact with her equine friends. Fumbling with the zip on yet another pocket she took out the torch, switching it on she waited until her eyes adjusted to the dim light. A magnificent black Arabian stallion was in the stall closest to her, its nostrils flared as he snickered and stamped the ground in protest at her presence. Reaching into another pocket she took out a mint, and patted the creature's glossy neck as it nuzzled its head into her in appreciation for the 'gift', she smiled and stroked the sleek healthy coat. "Good boy," she whispered, walking back into the middle of the barn and shining the torch towards the floor in front of her. Assuring herself that she was in the right spot, she shone the light around the building, then on the diagram showing her where Fiona thought she had dropped the bracelet. Getting down on her knees and standing the

torch on the floor she sifted through the sweet smelling straw. A rustle came from a dark corner and the brown mare nearest the noise shifted, she sucked in her breath and quickly turned her torch in the direction of the noise, her heartbeat quickened. Was it the police waiting for her? Her eyes caught sight of a field mouse as it scuttled through the straw, and she let out her breath. 'A mouse that's all!' she assured herself with relief, lowering her head she resumed her search for the missing bracelet.

"Is this what you're looking for?"
Her throat closed over, Kim was so startled she couldn't even scream as she knelt at the large well-shod feet of the owner of a deep husky masculine voice. No sooner had the words penetrated her ears, when lightening crackled around the stable followed by a mighty roar of thunder making the black horse whinny and stamp restlessly around. The voice spoke in a soft whisper using words she didn't understand, amazingly the large horse fell silent at his command!
"I asked if this is what you are looking for?" the growling voice asked again as his big hand came into the small circle of light, holding the gold bracelet under her nose. "Answer me," he commanded gruffly.
Finding her voice from somewhere she spoke softly as her eyes took in the contradiction of hardened working hands with long fingers and manicured nails before her, "Y-yes, but..."
"Get up!"
"I-I can't..." she whispered frozen with fear, she couldn't move!
With a guttural growl of impatience, his other hand caught her roughly under her arm and dragged her up unceremoniously.
Kim's blue eyes opened wide in amazement, he must be extraordinary tall because she was standing now and her eyes were level with his broad chest, his hand was still grasping her arm tightly. She chanced a quick glance up at his face and let out a whimper filled with dismay.
It didn't help that the torch lit his face from underneath, giving him a very sinister appearance, her heart thudded in her chest and her mouth went dry as she surveyed the most formidable man she had ever seen, stood before her. Her assailant was dressed totally in ebony, matching his raven black hair which was wet and slicked back austerely from his swarthy chiselled face, revealing a widow's peak, but the most terrifying thing about him was his eyes. They were almond shaped and golden, like a cat's, outlined by thick long black lashes. His dark winged brows were drawn into a frown over his slightly hooked nose, he looked dark and extremely dangerous, he reminded her of a panther or worse still, the devil incarnate! Who was he?

"P-please, l-let me g-go," she begged in a small stuttering voice that sounded nothing like her own, she tried to prise his long fingers off her bruised arm. "I-I'm not after the h-horses. I-I'm not a t-thief, y-you're hurting my arm!" she finished lamely.

Relaxing his hold a little his voice rumbled around the stable, "If you're not a thief, why are you looking for this, you stole it on an earlier visit to my home didn't you?" That's when he made his mistake, releasing his hold on her arm he held the bracelet up to her again.

Kim saw her chance of escape and sprinted towards the door. She didn't get very far before she felt his strong hands grab her around her arm and pull her back, "Oh no you don't lad! I've not finished with you yet," he bit out turning her around and grasping the collar of her jacket, yanked her against his strong hard body, his face so close she could see golden flecks in his tawny eyes.

For a moment Kim put up a struggle, which she knew she was fast losing as he dragged her back into the middle of the barn, her puny efforts lost on the powerful man. Then things took a turn, he let out a curse as his foot stepped on the torch she had left on the floor, and he lost his balance bringing her down with him onto a bed of hay.

Winded and shocked she gasped for breath as her chest hit his, before she could think he rolled them over, his massive body came down on top of her pinning her into the soft straw.

"You're a woman!" he stated in shocked surprise, as his body pressed into hers.

Heat flooded into her face, "So what?" she challenged, trying to ignore feelings that were alien to her.

"Ah, now I see," he uttered breathlessly enlightenment dawning, Trisha had spoken the truth, his voice softened a fraction and he shifted his weight off her a little. "You're not a thief, my brother gave you the bracelet I take it?"

'Why, his voice outdoes the thunder!' she thought a little hysterically. Now what did she say?

"Well? I'm waiting, at least have the decency to answer me woman!" he roared, causing his voice to resonate in her small chest. "You break into my stable, twice, then when I want to know why you are here, you remain silent. Perhaps you would rather talk to the police!"

"No! I-I came back for the bracelet, it means a lot and I wanted to find it," she told him truthfully, taking deep breaths to try to ward off the feeling of faintness that was threatening to envelop her, so this must be the formidable Seb!

A soft menacing laugh echoed around, "So Trisha for once in her sweet

life spoke the truth, Alex has got a lover!"
Kim looked away from his piecing golden eyes.
"The bracelet was once my mothers she gave it to Alex," he stated, as he turned it around in one hand somewhere above her head, stopping when he came to the clasp. "Ah, but the inscription indicates that it no longer belongs to him but to his...mistress," he purred with contempt as he stared down at her. "My mother would not have liked that!" His voice reverberated around. "You dropped it last night in your struggle with Alex's wife I take it?"
Flushing profusely she lowered her gaze, angry at being called a mistress, but unable to deny it because of giving Fiona away.
"Tell me, what am I do with you now? Alex is in no position to see you. His wife has already tried to murder you! Do I hand you over to the police, or..." there was silence for a moment, and Kim held her breath. "Or let you go I wonder?"
"P-please, yes, that would be awfully nice of you. I-I won't trouble you again," she assured him.
He threw back his head and roared with a mocking satirical laugh, revealing even white teeth, "How awfully polite!"
"Let me go!" she hollered crossly, realising he was playing a game of cat and mouse with her. "Do you hear me, get off me, I can hardly breath you're so heavy!" she grunted as she struggled under his incredible bulk. But he just stared at her, his breathing laboured and a look on his face that both scared and intrigued her. Self preservation made her stop struggling, as she became aware that her movements were causing more than a look of sensuality on his handsome face.
"Please d-don't hurt me..." she pleaded, her eyes filling with alarm as his hand reached out and pulled her hat off. The dark silky hair that was hiding under the hat spilt out like shiny black ink over the yellow straw.
"Believe me sweetheart, harming you is not on my mind," he whispered huskily as he stroked some dark strands off her camouflaged face, "have I hurt you?" His unexpected tender action caused her heart to thump so loud she forgot the horrendous storm overhead, it was nothing compared with the tumult that was going on inside her. It was as if he was hypnotising her, making her feel something she'd never felt before, taking away any power to resist. She was falling, drowning in those strange tawny eyes as they pierced into hers searching and touching her very soul, making her more afraid of the emotions that this man had somehow awakened within her than the situation she was in.
"Let me go!" she reasoned, aware that her eyes mirrored the desire he had roused within her.
"Oh Fiona, that's your name isn't it? Don't pretend you don't feel what

I'm feeling, I can see from the colour under all that black camouflage and those gorgeous blue eyes tell me different, did you know your eyes are the window of your soul?"

She shook her head causing her silky hair to brush his fingers, "Y-you a-are mistaken," she whispered feeling his fingers stroking the smooth strands.

"I don't think so, besides you are trembling and I can feel your heart beating against me," he teased, his clean cool heightened breath fanning her burning face.

Anger came to her rescue, "Some holy man you are!" She lashed out at him, her small fists hammering futilely on his shoulders and chest. "Of course you can feel my heart, you scared me...you're scaring me. Get off me you...you...you oaf!"

With ease he grasped both her small hands in one of his and held them above her head, laughing down at her he answered softly, "You scared? Now why don't I believe that, and why do you think I'm holy?"

Her eyes opened wider, now what should she say, "Alex said..."

"Alex," he smiled bitterly, "what has Alex said about me!"

"That you were studying to become a monk..."

"So I was!" he agreed his voice a gruff whisper. "But does that make me holy or for that matter immune to a lovely woman?"

"It should do!" she retorted.

His eyes were piercing into hers, amusement disappearing as another emotion took its place. "I can assure you I am all male, just ordinary flesh and blood, prone to sin as you and the rest of the world are. You are so beautiful." The pure unadulterated desire in his face left her in no doubt as to his next intention, he was going to kiss her! She sucked in her breath, she was in deep trouble, and there was only one thing she could do.

"You..." Her shoe came into contact with his shin and his face contorted with pain, "Ouch! You little vixen that hurt!" he grated.

Remorse swept over her at the thought of causing another pain, especially a man of God! "I-I'm sorry, I didn't mean to hurt you, but you did ask for it, just...just let me go...I won't tell anyone..." she whispered pleadingly her voice trailing as their breath mingled and grew heavier, and not just from the skirmish. As his eyes caught hers again time stopped still, he wasn't listening and everything around them had faded into oblivion, they were the only two people in existence, she lowered her eyes to his beautiful sensuous mouth only inches away from her lips. She heard him laugh seductively deep in his throat as he uttered, "Then I won't tell either!"

She shut her eyes and held her lips up to be kissed. Without a second

telling, his lips descended and claimed hers, setting her aflame and making her whimper in delight as she opened involuntary, inviting him to taste.
His kiss deepened when he met no resistance.

Neither heard the stable door as it creaked open, or saw the blue florescent light flicker on, but the sound of a softer masculine voice broke the moment, "Oh...Sorry Seb...excuse me I thought..."
"Alex!" Seb was on his feet in an instance and pulling her up roughly beside him, a scowl on his dark handsome face. 'How had this witch tempted him to do that?' he asked himself as he looked down at her with scorn. 'What was he thinking of, allowing his flesh to get the upper hand?'

Unable to hold his glare Kim looked down at the floor, and with shaky fingers touched her crushed and swollen lips, which still stung from his sensual touch. 'What had she done, he was a monk and she had enticed him, hadn't she? She must have, the venomous way he was looking at her, as if she was one of those women who were turned on by seducing men who chose to live a celibate life?' she thought to herself, feeling more than a little ashamed.
"Do you want me to go out and come back in again?" Alex asked in a tormenting tone, a big grin on his boyish face as he took in the predicament his brother was in. "Or would you rather I didn't come back at all?"
"No, don't be so ridiculous!" he pulled Kim into view so that his brother could see her, recognition settled on Alex's face when he saw Kim, then relief at Seb's next words.
"Fiona lost the bracelet you gave her and came back for it, I thought she was the thief so I wrestled her to the ground," he explained, his eyes still cloudy from passion.
Kim listened to him in disbelief as he quickly gained control of the awkward situation.
Throwing back his powerful shoulders and jutting out his blue chin, he reproached his brother. "Huh, I say thief, there was no thief was there Alex?" he stated pragmatically glancing from one to the other, once again fully in command, confident that his brother had swallowed the explanation.
"No," Alex admitted on a long sigh. Folding his arms across his chest he walked nearer to them, a myriad of emotions crossing his boyish features he quickly assessed the situation, aware that his brother had got the identity of the intruder wrong, and keen to take advantage of the

situation. "No, I'm sorry Seb, I was wondering how I was going to tell you. Fiona and I are lovers; we have been for over a year. I arranged to meet her here, she's staying at Rose cottage for a fortnight. We don't get much chance to see one another, what with Trisha being so...ill!" he grimaced shrugging his broad shoulders. "Perhaps now is as good as any time to explain."
"I wish you would," Seb invited.
Alex nodded then continued, "I think by now you know that I'm a battered husband!"
"I had my suspicions," Seb uttered, drawing his seductive mouth into a straight line.
"Well, eighteen months ago I left Trisha and filed for a divorce, mainly because of the injuries she was inflicting on me. It was during our separation that I met Fiona, it wasn't planned, I'd had my fill of women, or so I thought. My father-in-law's firm had dealings with Fiona's company, after one of many meetings I took her out for lunch, we became good friends...then the relationship deepened. Trisha found out I had someone else and took an overdose, I had no choice but to return. I felt sorry for her, and guilty that I'd driven her to that!" he smiled wryly. "One of the conditions of my return was that she receive treatment for her illness. This she did and Fiona and I tried to stay away from one another, we really did," he looked at his brother, willing the dark man to understand. Recognising a flash of compassion cross the austere face, he went on. "It worked for a while, then her mother started to interfere, telling Trisha that she didn't need help and that I was her problem...I was making her react violently and I should be the one receiving help!" Alex rubbed a frustrated hand across the back of his neck, and Kim's eyes filled up with tears, she stole a quick glance at Seb and sucked in her breath at the look on compassion that emanated from his face.
"Go on," Seb encouraged with warmth.
"Trisha refused her treatment and the abuse resumed. After a particularly bad attack I ran back to Fiona, she patched me up and looked after me until I'd recovered! We realised we were in love and started meeting secretly. I don't know how but Trisha found out that Fiona was coming down to the Island with me. She followed us down here, what I can't understand is how she knew where and what time I'd arranged to meet Fiona last night."
"She read your E-mail!" Kim chipped in.
Seb scowled at her, "You sent an E-mail to Alex's home?"
Kim lowered her head.
Alex came to her rescue. "It wasn't Fiona's fault, I asked her to reply to me that way, I mistakenly thought Trisha didn't have access to my laptop.

I normally have it with me, my mistake for leaving it in my study when I came here."
"I thought you seemed surprised when Trisha arrived last night!" Seb added.
"I was, I couldn't believe my eyes when she walked in! I should have realised she was up to something, she loathes this place! Anyway she'd found out about our tryst...she beat me to it," he stated whimsically touching his blackened eye and the bruising surrounding the lump on his forehead, "she knocked me out and waited for Fiona to arrive, you know the rest. Please Seb, don't give Fiona over to the police, she's no thief."

Seb walked over to the dark stallion, his back towards Kim and Alex, and spoke softy in that strange language to the animal, stroking it's long mane while he considered the young woman's fate and fought with his own conscience. He ought to tell his brother that the police were no longer looking for an intruder, but some devil inside him told him he could hold this over Alex. He needed Alex's co-operation to accomplish his own plans, besides something was amiss even between these two. Alex must have seen them kissing, the evidence was imprinted on her lips for all to see, but he hadn't reacted like a man in love, and the way she had just responded to his kiss, she certainly didn't love Alex. Why, she was no different from Trisha, and this time he was determined to stop history repeating itself!

Kim forced her eyes away from Seb's tall figure, her lips were still tingling from his burning kiss and her face was still very flushed. She shook the straw off her dishevelled hair and brushed herself down in an effort to appear normal. Heaven knew she didn't feel normal anymore! As if for protection she wandered over to stand by Alex. "Your brother thinks I'm Fiona," she murmured quietly, wincing as she got a closer look at the blonde man's injuries, amazed that a woman could have been responsible for such an assault!
Alex smiled, "I've gathered that, no wonder he looked so guilty when I caught the pair of you! If he was kissing Fiona as passionately, believe me he wouldn't be standing now!" he whispered back steering her behind a bale of hay. "Don't tell him you're not Fiona just yet, please Kim!"
"I-I don't know...I..."
"Please," he begged urgently, his face contorted with worry.

"Alex?" Seb called when he turned and looked at the empty space where they'd been standing.
"We're here," Alex answered his brother stepping back into his view,

"Please!" he hissed urgently over his shoulder at Kim.
Seb walked over to them; Kim noticed a dark flush staining his cheeks as he looked with disdain down his long nose at her. 'He thinks...we were...' she mused wondering why she felt so annoyed that he thought she was smooching with Alex behind the straw bales. His dark condescending look left nothing to the imagination of what he thought of her!
"I'll take Fiona home," Alex said, giving her no chance to speak out when he saw Seb's look.
"No," Seb reared into action. "I'm taking her back, the police are still around, it's best they don't associate Fiona with you for the time being, although we'll have to tell them eventually," he added for good measure. "I'll get the car while you explain what's happened since you last saw her!" he raised a perfect eyebrow and unhooked a coat hanging from a peg on the wall. Throwing the long black cape around his shoulders he turned to face her, the disdainful look still on his face.
Kim gasped and looked away, if he'd smiled she was sure she would have seen two fangs either side of his mouth!
"I won't be long, so be ready," he warned.

Kim sighed a sigh of relief as he disappeared in a flurry of black, the whole atmosphere lightened and she found she could breath more easily again.
"His looks belie his character, underneath that surly expression lies a pussycat!" Alex assured her when he took in her large frightened eyes.
Kim stifled a laugh as a vision of a black panther crossed her mind. "I'm sure he is," she agreed.
Alex sat down on a bale of straw and patted the one next to him. "Sit down, I'll tell you quickly what's happened then we'll get you home," he said frowning as he looked at his watch!"
Kim nodded as she lowered herself wearily next to the tall boyishly good looking blond man and looking into his blue eyes agreed, "I am rather tired."
"Please before Seb comes back, don't tell him who you really are, please trust me it's very important. I need to speak to Fiona. If he thinks you are Fiona, it will give me a chance to see her tomorrow. He obviously doesn't know you are staying with her, the cottage was only booked in her name, please Kim, please!"
Looking into his troubled face, she reluctantly agreed, "Alright, but only for now, after you have seen Fiona you must tell him the truth, and the police."
"I promise," he grinned crossing his heart with his hands. "Right, now

I'll tell you briefly what has happened. The ownership of the gun has been traced back to Trisha so the police know she's been lying. The police are awaiting a medical report before they charge her. Seb arranged a place in a secure private nursing home just outside Newport, don't look like that!" he begged as he studied her startled expression. "It was either that or a prison cell, he talked to the police and persuaded them that prison wasn't the answer in her state of mind. Seb has also organised a good solicitor for her."
Kim nodded sadly.
Alex took hold of her hand, "Please Kim, I'd appreciate your total silence for the time being, I can't tell you everything. I tried to give my marriage to Trisha a go, God knows I tried. I need to get away from her, for my own safety, because I fear that one day she'll go too far, or worse still, she will provoke me into retaliation. And because of yesterday, I now have Fiona's safety to consider!"
Kim shot him a look of compassion, the injuries to his face looked frightful, Trisha had given him an awful beating, and she must have knocked him senseless last night.
"That's why I need to see Fiona, I want to tell her that my marriage is through myself. It's unlikely that Trisha will be around for the next three years," he stated flatly. "So it will be easier, I never wanted it to end like this." He shook his head sorrowfully.
"Of course you didn't, she needs help, and fast, before she kills you or herself, at least she will get that now. How did Seb find out about me...I mean Fiona?"
"Until tonight I didn't think he knew about her." He laughed a satirical laugh, "Well at least I thought he didn't, but there, with Seb I should have known better, he seems to know everything," he mused frowning a little.
Kim shuddered, "Are you saying he's got powers to know things we don't?"
Alex laughed, "Wouldn't surprise me. I had no idea Fiona had dropped the bracelet!"
"She was worried the police would find it."
"I can understand that, the message I had engraved on it would have damned both of us, but why did you come here? You took an awful risk, you should have phoned and I could have looked for it."
"We didn't know if it was safe to phone you, Fiona didn't have the nerve to come again, Trisha really scared her, we didn't know Trisha...had gone...!"
"No, I should have got in touch, but the place was crawling with cops! They are still making enquiries in the area, you were lucky you weren't seen by them tonight!"

"Surely you mean it was lucky that I found the bracelet first and not the police," Seb's voice boomed making both of them look round.
"That's a point, where are the police?" Alex frowned suddenly realising an absence.
"You were very fortunate. The police suggested that the thief was unlikely to return to this property, I agreed and persuaded them not to leave an officer on duty here. I had a gut feeling that the intruder would return for the bracelet, and I wanted to catch him," he interrupted his brother. Then turning to speak to Kim, his sensuous lips curled in distaste as he took in their clasped hands. "Are you ready for home, it's been a long night and I for one am tired?"
"Yes," she smiled as she turned to Alex; it took her all her courage not to snatch her hand away, it was stupid but she felt she was being unfaithful to this strange man.
"It's best that Alex keeps away from you, at least until the police activity in this area dies down, unless you desire to tell them the intruder was you!" Seb suggested sarcastically, his face a stern mask. "They might charge you with wasting valuable police time!"
"I didn't call them, you did!" she snapped back.
"For good reason, now if you're ready?"
"I'll say goodnight then Alex," she said ignoring the note of censure.
A look of amusement crossed Alex's face, he had never seen Seb so rattled since they were boys. Smiling he stood up, effectively barring his brother from her, "Er...excuse us brother!"
Seb snorted and marched towards the door leaving them alone to say goodnight.

When he'd gone, Alex pulled her towards him and chastely kissed her cheek. "Thanks for not giving us away."
"It's only until you've seen Fiona, why are you laughing at me?" she questioned suddenly seeing the merriment in his face.
"Have you looked in a mirror recently. Who made your face up?"
"Fiona," she said touching her face, she'd forgotten about the dark streaks, she must look a sight! "My face was too luminous for night work so she darkened it!"
"I hope it's not boot polish, it'll never come off!" Alex stated horrified.
"No, it's only make-up," she giggled back.
"Thank heavens for that you look extremely ferocious!"
"Not half as ferocious as your brother!" she blurted out. "Oh! I'm sorry I shouldn't have said that!"
Alex's eyes crinkled with mirth as he hooked her arm in his and led her towards the door. "Really he's not an ogre, he's taken me on as a partner

in his firm."
"But surely you have a right to half the estate anyway?"
"No, like the proverbial prodigal, I asked my father for my share years ago to set up my own business, Trisha spent it! Seb has given me a second chance, which is great, after she bankrupted me, I worked for my father-in-law, until today that is."
"Really? So there is a heart beating somewhere in the man!" she answered.
"Now, now," Alex admonished laughingly.
"Sorry, I'm sure under the circumstances working with him is a good move," she stated as they stepped outside, genuinely glad that the brothers had made up their differences.

When he saw them coming, Seb strode ahead towards the Range Rover, he had never felt so angry in all his life, what was his brother playing at? Wasn't it enough that one woman had fleeced him for everything he'd got! Couldn't Alex see what sort of a woman Fiona was, if he couldn't he would make damn sure that he did! Matching his mood, lightening flashed all around, his black cape billowed out after him as the wind caught it.

Kim shuddered as she looked at the formidable figure.
"Come on woman!" Seb shouted above the storm.
"Quickly you're incurring his wrath, goodnight and thanks," Alex stated giving her a small push towards the irate man.
"Goodnight Alex," she answered raising her voice as she ran to the door of the vehicle that Seb was holding open. He cupped her elbow as she climbed in; gasping she pulled away when a jolt of electricity ran through her arm from his touch, their eyes met for a short moment, had she imagined the look of shock on his face before he slammed the door after her?
Shivering, she watched him as he walked quickly round the front of the vehicle, the headlights giving him a foreboding look, she stiffened in fear as he opened his door and climbed into the driver's seat, did he possess unusual powers like Rasputin the mad monk?

"Is your belt done up?" he asked gruffly.
Turning she pulled at the strap, it wouldn't budge, she heard him mutter under his breath, and gasped as he leaned over her, his face inches away. She caught the now familiar tantalising smell of his tangy aftershave. "What are you doing?" she cried almost hysterically, his nearness causing her heart to beat an erratic tattoo.

"The strap is stiff?" he shouted above a loud rumble of thunder, his face set in a dark moody glare as he yanked the belt around her and clipped it into the anchor.
"I could have done it myself, I'm not a child!" she hissed resenting the fact that he was treating her like a small child.
"I am aware of that fact!" he stated grimly as he put the vehicle into gear.

Despite the awful weather the drive back only took a few minutes, the big four-wheeled drive vehicle took the flooded country roads with ease, and she reluctantly admitted to herself that he was a very competent driver. Embarrassed by the silence in the confined space Kim tried to strike up a conversation, but after a few minutes gave up when all she received were irritable grunts for replies. 'Pussycat indeed, he was more like a sourpuss!' she huffed keeping her eyes averted to stop her noticing his beautiful long hands as they gripped the wheel, even they had the ability to make her heart race.

Seb stopped the vehicle in an unmade road, hidden between some thick bushes. Pulling on the handbrake and turning the ignition off, he smiled sardonically at her gasp of fear, "Relax, I am able to resist you, and contrary to what you think I can assure you I'm not about to rape you!"
"I didn't think you were," she snapped indignantly, her cheeks glowing profusely at the thought.
He looked into her face and tutted, "I'm stopping here because if the police are about I don't want them led to the cottage until I can think of a feasible explanation, there's a footpath just ahead, it takes you to the front door of the cottage."
Kim glared at him before she unclipped her belt and opened the door jumping nimbly down onto the ground. Thanking him sarcastically for the lift she slammed the door shut.
"And I'm not the sort of woman who picks on sex starved priests!" she muttered indignantly under her breath. Pulling the zip to the jacket up to her chin, she stuffed her cold hands deep into the pockets, marched around the vehicle and headed down the dimly lit path towards the cottage, holding her head high, her face screwed up against the force of the driving rain. 'Despicable man!' she thought, for some strange reason feeling very near to tears. 'If he didn't want to take her back why on earth didn't he say. It wasn't as if she'd asked him for a lift!'

"Have you got the key?"
Kim's heart nearly stopped, she let out a small-strangled scream and

almost lost her footing, "Careful!" he warned reaching out and grasping her arm to steady her.
"You did that deliberately," she seethed shaking his hand off her and turning on him.
"Did what?"
"You scared me! I thought you'd gone!"
"I said I'd take you home," he commented a small devilish smile playing at the corner of his mouth when he saw that he'd startled her.
Kim saw the fiendish smile, wretched man he was enjoying this! "Oh very funny, creep up on a lady when she's walking on her own in the middle of the night, down a dark path, looking every inch like Count Dracula and give her a fright."
His face became stern again and she thought she saw anger flash in his eyes. "I'm truly sorry, I honestly thought you knew I was behind you."
"Well I didn't," she stated, huffing and turning she marched quickly away from him, smiling as he shouted irately after her.
"And I don't look remotely like Count Dracula."
"No? I thought that was your intention, you're dressed totally in black and you even wear a cape!" she threw back at him over her shoulder.
He caught up with her and pulled the collar of the cape up higher, "Weatherproof riding cape, useful in this climate, anyway you can talk, you're dressed totally in black. At least I didn't put black streaks on my face," he grinned broadly.
Kim stopped and gasped at the transformation his smile caused.
"Now what's wrong?" he asked frowning again as he stopped beside her, they had reached the cottage gate.
"You smiled!"
His smile turned to a chuckle. "Did my fangs show?"
Kim forgot to be cross and flashed him a smile back before she turned to unlatch the front gate. "Yes I think I caught a glimpse of them. Thank you for taking me home, goodnight," she stated dismissively.
"I'll leave when I've seen you safely in!"
'Drat, I wish he would go,' she thought as she fumbled through the concealed pouches of Fiona's jacket searching for the front door key, undoing each zip, 'if Fiona opens the door now!'

Seb watched her impatiently, uttering an oath under his breath. "You haven't lost the key?"
"I hope not! It may have fallen out of my pocket while we...while..."
"While we were romping around in the hay!" he finished a provocative smile playing on his luscious lips.
She chose to ignore his suggestive remark as she felt around in her

pockets, trying to still the erratic beat of her heart. "Ah, here it is!" she shouted, relief flooding through her as her fingers came into contact with the cold metal.
He took it from her and was just about to unlock the door, there was an enormous explosion of light accompanied by a splintering crashing sound. Kim screamed as his cloak flew around her, covering her completely, she was lifted off her feet by two strong arms and carried away, all she was aware of was darkness and the smell of his clean masculine body next to her face.
"What do you think you are doing?" she shrieked half shocked and half angry when he put her down, she struggled to remove her head from the confines of the cloak that was still covering her.
"What do you think I was doing, going for your jugular?" he muttered irately, staring intently over the top of her head his eyes held a far away look as he whispered, "Lady Rose".
"What? Oh!" she gasped pushing her dishevelled hair away from her hot face as she followed his gaze and looked behind her at the flaming branch that had fallen across the path where they had been standing.
The smell of burning material flooded her nostrils. He must have smelt it too; pushing her away he took off his smouldering cloak and brushed the burning embers from it.
"Thank you," she uttered shakily, realising that he had protected her from being burnt. "That could have..."
"It didn't," he dismissed, "Believe me it was more for self preservation, if I didn't get you safely back I wouldn't rate my chances with Alex. The lightening struck the oak tree. Are you alright?"
She nodded falteringly looking at the burning branch. "I think so."
"Good. Better put the fire out," Seb stated putting her to one side and walking back to the cottage, he opened the front door and wasted no time going into the kitchen and getting the fire extinguisher. Kim followed and filled a bucket with water willing Fiona to stay out of sight, she must be awake, surely no one would have slept through the noise that was made as the lightening struck the tree.

Kim put out the smaller fires that were burning in the grass from the sparks and left Seb to deal with the big branch. Satisfied that it was now safe he kicked the smouldering wood onto some gravel away from the cottage and wandered over to the stricken tree to examine the damage. "I'll arrange for a tree surgeon to come and check it tomorrow. Legend has it that when the oak dies, Lady Rose, whose spirit haunts the cottage, has returned in a new life to find her lover!" he turned and laughed. "Sorry, I shouldn't have talked about the ghost, you might be a little

nervous..."
"You aren't sorry, and at the risk of disappointing you I'm not in the least bit nervous, but I'm intrigued about the legend!" she interrupted. "Do tell."
"Some other time perhaps, it's far too late," he dismissed sharply, as he walked back into the cottage to return the extinguisher to the kitchen, beginning to regret saying anything about the myth. 'This sort of woman would use it to her advantage, and people were always ready to believe in such nonsense!' he reminded himself.
Kim shrugged off the intended rebuff and escorted him to the front door holding it open for him, "Fine, I'll ask Alex about it in the morning. Good night Seb and thank you for seeing me home safely."
He quirked an eyebrow at her blatant dismissal. "My pleasure, it's safe now and the storm is passing over, oh I nearly forgot," he grinned taking the bracelet out of his inside pocket and pushing it into her hand. "The reason for tonight! I'll bid you goodnight, do sleep well." Throwing his cape around his shoulders, he bowed low and left shutting the door firmly behind him.
Quickly Kim threw the bolts and rested her aching head on the wooden door, letting out a sigh of relief, 'thank goodness for that!

"Who was that, did you find my bracelet?" Fiona asked yawning as she walked sleepily down the narrow stairs. "I heard voices, you were gone ages so I went to bed, I thought you'd been arrested, I didn't know what to do!"
'So you did nothing!' Kim thought unkindly. "That was Seb, he found your bracelet, here," she said putting the item into her sister's hand, amazed that the metal hadn't scorched her.
"You've met Seb, did he help you find the bracelet, was Alex there?"
"Yes I met Seb, I've lots to tell you but tomorrow will have to do, I'm too tired to explain now," she told a startled Fiona as she stomped angrily up the stairs.
"But?"
"Not now Fiona, I said I'm tired!"

3

"Fiona, Fiona, I've overslept why didn't you wake me?" Kim called as she descended the stairs. "Fiona?" she repeated enquiringly a frown marring her lovely face as she poked her head around the kitchen door. It was empty but evidence that Fiona was up and had eaten stood on the kitchen worktop. Kim sighed as she put her sister's dirty dishes in the sink, she would wash them when she'd had her breakfast. Retracing her steps she went into the lounge, "Fiona." That too was uninhabited. She cast a disbelieving glance at the mantelpiece clock, it was almost twelve o'clock, 'what do you expect when you climb into your bed at two in the morning then stay awake until dawn thinking about the unobtainable?' she asked herself. Shrugging irritably as visions of Seb flashed before her eyes, groaning she returned to the kitchen, put the kettle on and popped two slices of toast under the grill before she took the butter out of the fridge. 'Fiona's probably gone for a walk,' she told herself looking out of the window, the weather was totally different from the last two days, it was a gloriously warm sunny spring day, not a cloud in the sky.

Humming a tune to herself she buttered her toast and took it into the lounge. It wasn't until she put the tray down on the coffee table that she noticed the envelope propped up against a vase, addressed to her in her sister's handwriting.
Frowning she opened it and took out the note, her eyes widening in disbelief as she read,

Dear Kim,

Alex came this morning and told me what happened

last night. His brother has taken him into partnership and sent him to Scotland for two weeks, under the pretext of dealing with a client, (more like, so that we don't get in touch with one another!). Can't be without him for that long so I've gone with him. Alex said Seb thinks you are me, so there is no need for him to find out I've gone with him.

See you back home, have a good holiday,

Fiona.

"What a nerve!" Kim said her hands shaking with rage, "Fiona, how could you? Grrrrr ..." she growled in anger. "How could you?" she ranted between gritted teeth as she tore the paper up into lots of little pieces and threw it in the bin. "Right now I hate you Fiona, you're a selfish...!"
A thought suddenly struck her, and she ran outside the cottage. Relief flooded through her, "Thank goodness!" she stated when she saw Fiona's car still standing on the drive. If Fiona had taken the wheels she would have been stranded, the nearest bus stop was miles away! As she turned to go back inside her eyes caught sight of the chard branch and the scorched grass. A wave of nausea swept over her as the truth hit her, if it had fallen on them they would both have been severely injured or worse! "How had Seb been so quick?" she shuddered as she remembered Alex's words hinting that he seemed to know more than others. Irritably she turned around and went inside. Her breakfast forgotten, she ran up the stairs, and stood staring into Fiona's room. 'How could I have missed it?' she wondered in disbelief as she looked at the empty wardrobe, Fiona hadn't even shut the wardrobe door.

Disappointment flooded her being, she had been looking forward to this break, entering her bedroom she took her case from the top of the wardrobe and laying it on the bed started packing, muttering irately to herself as she folded her clothes into it. "No point in staying now, damn you Seb Worsley, you've ruined my holiday, I might as well go home!"
"Why, because your lover has left?"
Kim let out a small scream and turned round startled. Looking devastatingly handsome in a navy suit, with a dark blue silk shirt and tie, Seb walked confidently into the bedroom.
"Oh you!" she gasped breathlessly, covering a shaking hand over her

thumping heart, glaring at the intruder. "I might have known it was you! How did you get in here?"
"If I told you I flew in through the open window, you'd believe me," he grinned wickedly revealing perfectly shaped white teeth.
"Don't be stupid," she muttered, making him laugh as she looked suspiciously at the window. "Would you mind leaving."
The laughter disappeared and his face became a dark brooding mask as his eyes raked over her, he didn't take too kindly to the condescending way she spoke to him. "You left the front door wide open, I did call but you were too busy talking to yourself to hear, I don't usually enter a property uninvited, unlike you!" he accused.
Kim had the grace to blush.
"That aside, I need to discuss something with you," he said leaning nonchalantly against the wall and folding his arms across his broad chest as he watched her pack, seemingly unaware of the tension crackling around them.
"Well I've nothing to say to you!" she replied huffily aware that he'd somehow turned the tables on her, just like he had last night when Alex had come into the stables.
"Believe me, it's for your own good that I sent Alex away, you might have been tempted to see one another, under the circumstances I don't think that's a good idea. In the early hours of this morning the police caught a gang of horse thieves who were operating in the next village. I'd hate them to think you were one of them!"
Tutting she took a pair of trousers off a hanger and turned away from him as she folded them neatly on top of the other clothes. 'So Fiona was right he had deliberately sent Alex away to separate them!' "You know I'm not a thief, and it's none of your business if Alex and I see one another, he's old enough to make his own decisions, he's thirty-one!" she snarled snapping her case shut and attempting to lift it off the bed.
"Allow me," he said his large hand taking the handle from her, she snatched her hand away quickly trying to avoid contact.
Aware of her evasive action, he smiled putting her mood down to a fit of pique because her lover had gone. "The pair of you haven't much sense, I wouldn't put it past Trisha to try and make trouble for you both. At the moment, because of her present state, the police aren't taking too much notice of what she's saying."
"If she's locked up in this nursing home how would she know what Alex and I are up to?"
"She was born on the Island, her family live just outside Freshwater, and they will stop at nothing to try to condemn Alex. There is not much love lost between our two families, besides this is a small island, gossip

thrives."
Kim raised her eyebrows.
"Believe me Trisha's family are not nice people, and the appearance of a beautiful woman meeting with her husband might just give them the ammunition they need. Anyway Alex may be thirty-one but he's still a bad judge of character."
"What do you mean by that?" she asked prickling with indignation, he was insulting her...well Fiona.
His face became an unreadable mask,
"You know full well what I mean sweetheart, he's still a married man. You may be able to pull the wool over Alex's eyes, but you sure don't fool me lady, and I'll do everything in my power to make Alex see you for what you are! You are not the right one for him, like Trisha you'll end up hurting him."
"How dare you, I'd never resort to violence!"
"My shin wouldn't agree with you," he grimaced.
"That was self-defence, h-how did I know y-you weren't some...some...perv... maniac?" her voice receded to a whisper as she read the disdain in his eyes.
"You didn't, but may I remind you it was my property you broke into."
"I didn't break into it, the door was open, and I was there because Alex...!"
"Please," he grinned suddenly holding up a hand as he remembered why he'd come. "Truce. I haven't come here to argue, and I didn't mean you would physically hurt him, but we both know you don't love him and he doesn't love..."
"Oh no, and what would you know about love?" she prevaricated, knowing he was being very astute, she didn't love his brother, but Fiona did, if he saw the love in Fiona's eyes when she spoke of Alex then he'd change his mind.
For a split second his face clouded over and Kim thought she saw a flicker of pain in his eyes, before he shook his head, as if he were struggling to erase some vision that had flashed before him. "Enough to know that when a woman loves a man, she doesn't enjoy another man's kisses, and if Alex really loved you I wouldn't have been standing when he came into the barn last night!" he answered softly.
"I don't know what you're getting at!" she answered groaning inwardly, colour flooded into her cheeks as she remembered the way she'd responded to his kiss, 'no invited it,' she chastised herself, the circumstance she was now in was to some extent her fault, she was very attracted to him!
His hand cupped her chin, lifting her face up to his, "Sweetheart, you and

I know you invited the kiss and you enjoyed it, your colour gives you away. The lack of concern on your lover's part too, spoke volumes!"
Kim pulled away from his hold and turned her back on him, "Alex didn't see, h-he thought we were...t-thought you were...trying to stop me from leaving," she finished falteringly.
She heard his deep guttural laugh. "Really?" he scoffed with disbelief. "I'll take this downstairs for you." Not waiting for a reply he left with the case.

Kim stood glaring at his arrogant retreating figure, Fiona and Alex had put her into an impossible situation, but if she told him the truth now, another feud would erupt between the two brothers and Alex didn't need anymore problems. She had no choice but to carry on with this stupid charade.

Following him down the stairs she stomped down hard in a very unladylike fashion, just to let him know how angry she was. Deep down inside she knew he was right in saying Fiona should keep away for a while, she would have given her sister the same advice, but it would be the last thing she'd admit to this haughty man. But he was wrong about their feelings, she was sure they really were very much in love. The sooner they told Seb the truth the better. 'When he saw them together he'd have to eat humble pie!' she thought elatedly, 'and I'd like to be around when he did!'

Seb put her case down in the hall and turned just in time to see her childishly poking her tongue out at him. The glimmer of a smile was soon wiped out by a frown, but he said nothing as he watched her descend the stairs, through narrow golden eyes. She felt his gaze wandering over her and she faltered a little, he reminded her of an eagle watching his prey, his eyes were certainly the right colour!
Reaching the last but one step she stopped, and thrusting out her small pointed chin, crossed her arms over her chest. Mainly because his large frame was blocking her way and it would mean her having to brush past him, and she was very aware that any physical contact with this man would be dangerous. Besides, she felt it was better to have an elevated position, that way she could look him in the eye, well almost.
"I'm not leaving here..."
His brow rose as he looked down at her case.
"I mean...not yet. I've not had breakfast...er...I got up rather late," she explained as he shot her a confused look. 'Heavens his very presence made coherent thinking and speaking impossible.' "I'm not travelling on

an empty stomach for anyone, and anyway I've paid the rent on this cottage for a fortnight. Or have you persuaded the owner's to turf me out?"

His golden eyes bore rudely into hers, "Why should I do that?"

"You sent Alex away," she accused him.

"I needed him to do some business..."

"Oh come on you can do better than that, *Sir* Worsley!"

A dark flush fused his cheeks at her obvious insult, and as she looked into his golden eyes she saw his pupils dilate in anger and her bravado increased, she'd managed to rattle his cage. She could tell that he wasn't used to people arguing with him!

"The name's Seb, and can I remind you that you were packing when I came, I'm not turning you out and for the record I *am* the owner of this cottage."

"Oh!" was all she could find to say, that did it she was definitely leaving.

He continued, "You don't have to leave on my account, but correct me if I'm wrong, I distinctly heard you say there wasn't much point in staying!"

"Because I am now on my own! Would you like to take a holiday in a remote cottage on your own?"

"Strange as it may seem Fiona, I'd love it!" he replied wearily. "Now will you listen to what I have come to say to you?"

Kim was glad he'd called her by her sister's name, in her anger she'd quite forgotten she was supposed to be Fiona.

"No, I would rather you went, I'll have lunch then I'll get out of your sight. Where shall I leave the key or did you want to do an inventory to make sure I've not stolen anything?"

Something snapped in the big man. "God you're the most exasperating woman I have ever had the misfortune to meet. I said I wanted to discuss something with you!" he growled at her.

"And I said I wasn't interested in what you have to say. I realise by your reaction that people don't usually question your orders, but here's one who does. Excuse me," she snapped waspishly back, taking the last step and brushing past him knocking him against the wall of the narrow hall.

In an instant, his long fingers curled around the top of her arm holding her back, she looked down at his hand then up at his face with utter scorn, "Let go, didn't anyone tell you that's no way to treat a lady?"

"Sweetheart, from what I've seen and know of your behaviour you're no lady!" he sneered.

"And if I'm not behaving like a lady it's because you're no gentleman!" she pouted back stung by his obvious abhorrence of her, she longed to tell him she wasn't the kind of woman he thought she was. "Let go!" she demanded.

"Gladly," he spat out angrily, noticing the moisture welling up in her eyes he released her. "The last thing I need at the moment is a blubbering woman on my hands," he muttered running an exasperated hand through his thick black hair.
Kim turned her back on him and took deep breaths in an effort to stem the threatening tears, annoyed that he'd seen them.
"I'll put your case in the boot of your car, where are the keys?" he barked more than a little shocked by his own aggressive action, she sure brought out the worst in him!
"In my bag, I'll go and get them," she answered shakily.

Thankfully he didn't follow her into the lounge but waited in the hall, it gave her time to control her shattered emotions. Kim rubbed her bruised arms, 'I hate you!' she lied.
Rummaging in her bag a cold feeling crept down her spine, Fiona had driven them to Osborne House yesterday...Fiona still had the keys! "Damn," she uttered in frustration between clenched teeth, throwing her handbag down on the chair.
"Something wrong?" Seb asked, coming into the room.
"I haven't got the keys!"
"You've misplaced them?"
"N-no, I've..."
"Lost them?" he asked with a condescending air, he might as well have added, what more could you expect from a mere woman! "Alex has taken the BMW otherwise I'd offer to loan it to you. I'll phone your garage and arrange for them to order another set of keys."
A feeling of despair crept over her, if she allowed him to do that he could find out she wasn't Fiona.
"It's not mine...er...it belongs to a friend, she loaned it to me!" she wailed, "I'm stuck here in the middle of nowhere, without a vehicle...on my own...and it's all your fault!"
Seb frowned, "My fault, how have you managed to come to that conclusion?"
"If you hadn't sent Alex away..."
"You could have played the harlot while his wife was locked away?" he suggested, his eyes flashing disapproval. "Doesn't it bother you that he's a married man? You could at least have the decency to wait until he's divorced!"

An ominous silence fell, and Kim hung her head, stung by his unfair accusation, but what could she say? An inward struggle ensued as she came very close to defending herself and telling this man the truth. For the life of her she didn't understand why, but it really bothered her that he thought so little of her! Then Alex's plight came to her mind. Instead she muttered, "Wasn't it William Penn who said, 'Never despise what you don't understand!"

For a moment he was silent, then he sighed and raised his hand up in the air in an act of surrender.

"Yes, I'm sorry, as you so rightly said, it's none of my business and I shouldn't judge you. That was unkind, the last few years can't have been easy for Alex, but believe me I have his best interest at heart, and yours for that matter, if you took this relationship further you would both end up hurt. Look, I think under the circumstances it would be best if you lodged in the Manor House, at least until you phone your friend for replacement keys."

"My friend is on holiday, I don't know the address!"

"That settles it then, I don't like the idea of you staying here alone, anyway Alex asked me to look after you, he would never forgive me if I left you here without transport or any means of communication!"

Her mouth dropped open, what was Alex thinking of asking Seb to look after her. The full extent of their deceit hit her hard. "Thanks for the offer but, no thanks, as you so rightly put it, what would the police say if a beautiful...I-if I turned up at the Manor now, they will start asking awkward questions. Alex had no right to ask that of you, I'm big enough to look after myself."

His face softened, "You are? You have already lost your friend's car keys! Anyway I doubt the police will think anything amiss, you would be my guest, it would be diff..."

"I don't see why," she interrupted.

"I often have friends visiting me."

"I bet you do!" she replied sarcastically. He had the nerve to question her morals and this was a man of the cloth? Somehow the thought of him entertaining women irked her.

Ignoring her outburst he went on to explain. "Trisha's family would think nothing of it when it got back to them that I was entertaining a beautiful woman," he smiled, "but they might if they were told Trisha's husband was meeting you, I'm unattached, that's the difference!"

"I'm leaving, I'll get a taxi to the ferry terminal."

He shrugged his broad shoulders, "Just as you like, I can't make you stay, I'll tell Alex you refused my offer of hospitality, I'd volunteer to drive you to the ferry but," he pulled back his suit sleeve, "I've got a meeting in just over an hour's time."

"How far is the terminal from here?"

"Just under an hours drive," he told her.

"An hour! How far is it?" she asked adding up the cost of a taxi in her mind, Fiona was looking after their cash! 'Surely it hadn't taken them that long to drive here?' she frowned, it had taken them almost an hour but she had assumed that was because they had got a little lost, it had been dark when they drove off the ferry at Fishbourne.
"About twenty-five miles away." 'There and back, it probably was!' he justified the small lie to himself!
"I'll walk to the bus stop, or perhaps you have time to drop me there?"
"No good," he smiled a look of apology on his handsome features. "There is only one bus in the morning and one in the evening, you've missed it!" he lied again.
"I'll call a taxi."

Ignoring the knowing self-satisfied look that crossed his handsome face, Kim thumbed through the yellow pages, then picked up the phone and held it to her ear.
"It's dead!" she stated looking at the silent receiver then accusingly back at him.
A feeling of elation shot through him as he regained control of the situation. "The storm brought down the telephone lines when it hit the tree, that's one of the reasons I wanted to talk to you, the telephone engineers should be fixing it tomorrow!" he replied walking over to her, taking the receiver off her and putting in back on the cradle. "Look I really don't want you to stay here alone, especially as you have no means of contact should an emergency arise. Come on, I'll treat you to lunch then drop you off at the Manor House, if you still don't want to stay until we get another set of keys for the car, I'll run you to the boat."
"I thought you said you had a meeting?" she reminded him accusingly picking up her discarded breakfast things.
"I have, at the Manor House at two o'clock, I'll take you to the ferry after, leave them," he indicated to the plate of toast in her hand, I'll send my maid over to clear up!"

Without a backward glance he picked up her case and walked out to his vehicle putting it in the boot. "Come on, I really haven't got an awful lot of time," he shouted over his shoulder as he hid his mobile phone in the glove compartment and locked it, a wicked smile pulled at the corners of his mouth, this was a Godsend. If he could get her to stay it wouldn't take long to convince her she wasn't in love with Alex after all!
Kim mumbled a surly 'thanks' as she got into the Range Rover and put the cottage keys on the dashboard.
"Pub lunch do?" he asked ignoring her sullen mood.

"Admirable," she answered miserably pulling the seat belt around her with ease this time.

The pub he took her to was very quaint nestled in Tennyson's Down overlooking the English Channel, despite her earlier bad mood Kim found herself looking forward to tasting the appetising food that was on display. The delicious smells wafting under her nose fired her hunger making her mouth water and her tummy rumbled, reminding her that she had missed breakfast.
"Is this place alright?" Seb asked watching her intently.
"Fine," she replied, wishing she could say the same about the company, although she had to admit, he didn't look so formidable in the daylight! His hair wasn't sleeked back and plastered against his face. In fact it was shiny and a little wavy, and no matter how many times he pushed it back, an errant lock kept falling over his brow, she swallowed as a desire to brush it back with her hands came over her. She frowned and quickly looked away.
Seb chuckled and whispered softly in her ear, "Give in Fiona and appease your growing hunger!"
"Pardon?" she asked turning back to him aghast, had he read her thoughts?
"You looked at the food, then frowned, Alex told me you watched what you ate! Surely eating one good meal won't spoil your delightful figure, besides you're on holiday?"
"Oh! Y-yes," she lied colouring at his compliment about her figure, Fiona always watched what she ate. Something she didn't, her work was so demanding and physical she didn't need to! "I didn't have breakfast so I'm owed a few calories!"
"Good," he smiled cupping her elbow and leading her into the dining area, "I can't abide skinny woman anyway!"

It was busy but Seb soon found them a table, "What's your poison?" he asked as she sat down.
"White wine please."
"Dry or sweet?"
"Dry."
"Of course, less calories!" he smiled and walked over to the bar.

Kim picked up a menu and studied it while she waited for him to return.
"You won't need that!" he stated taking the menu off her. "I've ordered the local speciality, I know you'll enjoy it. You can't come to this

establishment and not try the cook's home-made beef pie, this is local wine too!" he stated putting her glass of wine down and taking the seat opposite.
"You're very presumptuous ordering me beef pie, I might be a vegetarian!" she answered.
His eyes swept over her beautiful face, "I know you are not."
"How?" she questioned.
"Alex again, I'm afraid, he talked none stop about you when I got home last night, I feel I almost know you!" he said dryly.
"Oh," Kim answered lost for words, now what did she do? If Alex had told him things about Fiona, she would have to be careful not to contradict what he'd said. 'Oh what a tangled web we weave,' she mused.
"Now," he looked at her apologetically, "Would you mind if I go over some papers that I need to look at before my meeting. It will only take a few minutes then you can have my undivided attention!" he smiled wickedly at her.
Kim shrugged, "I don't mind in the slightest and I can assure you the last thing I need is your exclusive attention, please go ahead."
"Thank you," he answered ignoring her rudeness and getting the papers out from his briefcase.
It suited her, the less they conversed the less likelihood there was of her giving the game away. She found it very difficult pretending to be Fiona and embarrassing when he'd asked her things about Alex that as a lover she ought to know. On the drive to the pub, he fired question after question; it was almost as if he were trying to trip her up. 'Still,' she told herself, 'she'd handled it well, and in another few hours she'd be out of his sight, for good!'

Seb got engrossed with the papers in front of him, and when her eyes had adjusted to the dim light, she took advantage of looking around her delightful surroundings. It was a typical English country pub, and like so many were becoming these days because of drink driving, it was more like a restaurant. Despite the fact that it was a warm spring day, the large fireplace had a roaring fire, which was needed as the building was made of stone and wasn't overly warm. Noting a pair of masculine eyes looking at her from the other side of the room, she coloured and turned her attention back to the man in front of her. To her surprise he was glaring ferociously back at the man, then at her.
"Friend of yours?" he spat out sarcastically.
"N-no, of course not!" she replied indignantly.
He shook his head and muttered under his breath before he returned to his notes.

"Look it's not my fault he was staring at me."
Seb looked up, his golden piercing eyes searching hers, "Oh come on Fiona, I'm sure you are very well aware of your impact on men."
"What do you mean by that?" she uttered resentfully.
"Why nothing, except that a woman with your looks...and the way you dress..." his eyes roved insolently down and stopped at the top of her low cut blouse.
"I'm going to the ladies," she snapped pushing back her chair and picking up her bag.
She heard his sardonic laugh as she walked away from the table. "Insufferable man!" she fumed under her breath.

When she had calmed herself down she returned to the table, relieved that he didn't even look up from his notes as she sat down again. Not daring to look around the place anymore in case she caught anyone else's eye, she studied the man in front of her. A little surprised she noticed a sprinkling of grey hairs at his temples, 'was he much older than Alex? Surely not, the only lines on his rugged face were laughter lines around his eyes. Laughter lines! Had he got a sense of humour after all?' she mused. A frown furrowed his high forehead pulling his winged eyebrows together as he concentrated on his papers, then as if suddenly aware that he was being observed he looked up and caught her staring.
"Something wrong?" he asked, his tawny eyes holding hers.
Flushing she shook her head, "Y-you were frowning at your papers," she offered lamely.
"Umm...It's a report from my vet, it's a little technical, a horse I am taking on has medical complication," he said putting the papers back in his case.
"Taking on?"
"Yes, my main business is in the running of the estate, but I keep a small area on the farm for unwanted farm animals, sort of 'zoo' for underprivileged city kids and children with disabilities. Schools from all over Britain bring youngsters from the city centres for a break." he grinned. "Some of the kids don't know that milk comes from cows!"
She grinned back; "I can well believe it. That's a wonderful thing to do."

Kim watched his face became animated as she fired questions about the 'zoo' at him, and she knew she had touched his heart. "How long have you done that for?" she asked genuinely interested.
"Six years, a friend of mine works on the mainland with autistic children, she used to bring the children to the farm at weekends. We found the animals helped them to communicate so I've decided to expand, turn it

into a rescue centre. Not just for the children, many wild animals need a little care after injuries, and they would benefit. My goal is to build an operating theatre for horses, we haven't anywhere on the Island, sick horses have to be transported to the mainland, the stress of a long journey lessens their chances of recovery!"

Unable to help herself she pushed further, for some reason she had to find out more, not about the farm, but about the friend. "I hope you achieve it, do you and your...er...friend run it together?"

He leant forward and clasped both her hands in his, for a brief moment she saw sadness cross his handsome features. "You are asking if Louise and I are an item," he perceived, his all-seeing eyes probing deeply into hers.

"Certainly not!" she lied, trying to free her hands. "I-I just wondered if..."

"Liar!" he mocked, "your face is an open book."

Any feeling of compassion she had, quickly dissipated, "Think what you like, I was just trying to be friendly," she rasped giving a tug at her hands in an effort to free them. "Perhaps I can help decipher your papers. I'm..." she stopped herself just in time, she was just about to tell him she was a veterinary surgeon. "I'm used to vet reports, Alex probably told you I was a veterinary nurse before I worked for an engineering firm." she explained holding her breath and mentally crossing her fingers at her deliberate lie. He looked at her intently for a moment. 'Well Fiona had,' she told her conscience indignantly. Fiona had worked at the practice with her, until she decided to change careers and study engineering. It was safe to admit that, Fiona was no fool and had picked up the medical side very quickly, in fact Kim's senior partner had tried to persuade Fiona to go back to university and study to become a vet.

"You were an animal nurse? Alex didn't tell me that!"

"My twin and I followed Daddy into the veterinary business, he's got a country practice in Surrey," she answered truthfully managing to evade a direct lie.

For a moment he just looked at her then released her hands. "See if you can enlighten me then," he challenged, tossing the papers across and pointing to a paragraph. "What does that mean?"

Kim spent a few minutes deciphering and explaining the notes for him.

"So in your opinion, you think I should still take the creature on?"

"Certainly the hoof infection, Laminitis, is the most serious thing wrong with him, it is a common enough problem."

"I was more concerned about the report on his back."

"The problem has been caused from ill fitting saddles and the only limitation would be that the children wouldn't be able to ride him."

"He would be too big for them. I have other smaller ponies and donkeys for that purpose. I would like to show him to the kids though and maybe hire him for a stud.

"Good idea, his hoof problem can be controlled by a farrier and medication, and wouldn't effect his ability to breed, its not too expensive to treat, nothing that you couldn't afford that is."

"Oh and how would you know what I could afford!" he asked raising his brows and gathering the papers together, his features settled into a mistrustful scowl, 'Was that it, was this women after his brother's money? Perhaps he could pay her to keep away from Alex, maybe he would try that if nothing else worked!'

"I-I don't, I only assumed. I'm sorry, I was very rude, I didn't think," she uttered looking down, goodness did he see her as a gold digger, is that why he was against Alex and her...Fiona?

"Apology accepted. You are extremely knowledgeable about horses," he acknowledged a questioning frown marring his brow, he put the report away as their food arrived.

"Not really, the practice I work...worked at, dealt mainly with small animals, but we treated the odd equine, mainly pet ponies. I enjoy my...I enjoyed working with John Staten the vet," she amended, thinking that at this moment she could cheerfully strangle Fiona and Alex for putting her in this awkward position.

"It shows," he answered raising his eyebrows. "Just one thing I don't understand is if you enjoyed it so much, and your face tells me you did, why move on to engineering?"

Kim looked stunned for a moment desperately searching her brain for an answer, then said the words that Fiona had told her father. "My family eat, breathe and sleep vet..."

"And you wanted to be different, choose your own vocation?" He offered her a way out.

Kim nodded and winced at the note of frustration and torment in his next words.

"Well nice if you can do it," he stated under his breath with more than a little frustration. "Now enough questions, tuck in and tell me what you think of the local fare."

4

Seb left her in his lounge, sitting on one of the two large green sofas, her feet sinking into the soft Chinese carpet. "Elsa, my maid, will bring you a drink, I'll be as quick as I can," he said shutting the door and leaving her alone.

"My maid no less!" Kim mimicked his cultured accent as she looked around the magnificent room, where the layout had managed to blend modern designs with the old. It was very beautiful, not what she had expected. What had she expected? A very sparse masculine home, especially if he'd spent time in a monastery! Didn't the church erroneously teach that comfort was not what God wanted for his children? Well if they did Seb had other ideas. This smacked of opulence and a woman's touch. Probably their mother's, perhaps the woman friend he had spoken about earlier had been responsible. Kim frowned at the idea and a flash of emotion suspiciously like jealousy caught at her; she quickly pushed the feeling down, not daring to analyse it. A restlessness swept over her, she wished she'd taken a taxi now, she could have tried the phones in the pub, they might have been connected. It was dangerous being in the man's company, already he seemed to have some sort of a hold on her that both thrilled and frightened her. Sighing, she walked over to the large stone fireplace and picked up a silver framed photograph, it was of an older couple and two teenage boys, looking closer she realised it was Alex and Seb with their parents. Replacing the frame she smiled, like her and Fiona, Seb was like his father and Alex his mother. Another photo caught her attention, it was of Seb dressed in black trousers and black shirt, standing beside a nun, it was signed, 'to my darling friend Seb, love Lou'. Kim felt that same emotion return and tug inside her as she studied the young woman's face, so this was his friend,

she was extremely serene and beautiful, they were laughing and the eye contact was there for all to see! Her brain worked overtime trying to fathom why his face showed pain at the mention of her name. 'Had they met while he was in the monastery and fallen in love? His attire certainly looked like priests clothing! Or had she left him to join Holy Orders?' she pondered.
Kim nearly dropped the frame as the maid came in with a tray, "Would you like your drink in the lounge, or out on the patio Ma'am?"
"Here would be fine," Kim answered putting the photo down.
The curtains moved gently in the breeze, the open French windows beckoning her to explore the garden. "No perhaps if you don't mind, I'll have it outside," she murmured, "its such a beautiful day, and quite warm for the time of year."
"It certainly is Ma'am," the young woman smiled taking the tray outside.
Wandering over to the door she stepped outside onto a large patio covered with pots of perfumed plants in an array of glorious colours.
"I didn't realise this house was so near the sea!" Kim gasped in awe as she stood by the balustrade and took in the vista of blue sea sparkling in the spring sunshine.
"The garden backs onto a private beach, if you listen you can hear the waves on the shore," the maid answered and waited for Kim to settle herself on a cushioned lounger. She smiled and put the tray down on the table next to her, "Is there anything else I can get you, Ma'am?"
The woman left after she assured her that she was fine. Soon the effects of the water lapping the shore, warm sun, a sleepless night, and a large meal took effect and Kim drifted off to sleep.

Voices coming from the lounge woke Kim from her nap. Recognising Seb's deep husky tones and realising he was heading her way she sat upright, quickly trying to smooth down her crumpled short skirt and combing her fingers through her tousled hair trying to put it into some sort of order.
Seb walked out onto the patio and cast her a sensuous glance as he took in her crushed skirt that revealed more of her long shapely legs than she would have liked. He wasn't alone, another man whose face was hidden behind the glare of the sun stepped out after him.
"Ah, here you are, we thought we would join you for a drink before..."
"Kim! Kimberly Brennan, well I never!" the other man interrupted Seb in surprise, walking towards her his hand extended in friendship. "Fancy meeting you here!"
Seb frowned, "You know one another?"

Standing up and shielding her eyes from the sun so that she could see who the other person was, her heart fell, he was one of her tutors from university. Kim thought and thought fast, it was nearly six years ago, and she had changed a little, her hair was longer and she used to lighten it in an effort to look more like Fiona. She had also lost what her father had kindly called, her 'puppy fat!'

"Why yes, it's Kim, Kim Brennan, I taught you at veterinary college do you remember?"

She held her breath and crossed her fingers behind her back, not daring to even glance in Seb's direction. "I'm sorry Sir," she answered with a convincing frown on her lovely face, hating herself for the deceit, and trying to word it so that she didn't actually lie. "I have a twin, much to my father's consternation only one of us went to veterinary school and became a vet!"

"This is Fiona Brennan," Seb introduced her again.

"Ah, that explains it, twins! Well I'm pleased to meet you Fiona, my name is Paul, Paul Adkins, and forgive my mistake, you are very like your sister, though now I can see the subtle differences!"

Kim smiled and took hold of the man's extended hand, "How do you do, Mr Adkins."

"Paul, please, where's Kim working now?" he asked hitching his trousers and taking a seat next to her.

Kim gradually relaxed and even managed to hold a normal conversation, cleverly bringing the discussion round to safer ground. Seb eventually sat down with them but didn't join in, his face set in a mask, as he listened, did he suspect?

Relief flooded her when Paul finished his drink and stood up to leave, "Well it's been nice meeting you Fiona, do give my regards to Kim," he said shaking hands again.

"I will, and it's been a pleasure meeting you Paul," she replied casting a furtive look at Seb. He was still watching her so intently it unnerved her, what was it Alex had said, 'With Seb I should have known better, he knows everything!'

Kim shuddered at the thought, causing Seb to narrow his eyes at her before he turned to Paul, "I'll walk you to your car, I'd like you to take a look at Susie, I think she has a problem. I'll be back!" he threw menacingly over his shoulder to Kim.

When he'd gone, she sank down wearily on the sun bed, 'What a mess,' she thought miserably as she waited for Seb to return.

'Where was he?' she wondered glancing at her watch, she'd been waiting half an hour, surely it didn't take that long to see the other man off. A noise the other side of some bushes at the end of the patio caught her attention. It was a dog and it seemed to be in some distress. Hurriedly she followed the sounds and stepped through a small opening between two yellow forsythia bushes.

"What are you doing?" she shouted.

Seb was leading a reluctant Rottweiler across to the stables, and it clearly wasn't very happy, "I said what are you doing?" she demanded crossly running over to the distressed dog.

Seb stopped and glared at her.

"Oh you poor thing!" she exclaimed sinking to her knees beside the disturbed Rottweiler. "What's he doing to you?" she asked the animal patting its velvety head.

"Meet my dog Susie, she gave birth to ten puppies yesterday, and has now developed a milk infection. Paul has put her on a course of antibiotics and I can't allow her pups to suckle for two days! Despite what you think, I'm not doing anything to her, other than helping her. And I resent your inference! Now if you'll excuse me," he rasped impatiently.

"I never thought you were, I..."

"For your information, if I allowed the pups to feed from her they'd be seriously ill!" he replied scornfully. "But of course you would know that!"

"Of course, I know...I didn't mean..."

He sighed, the angry look left his face and he seemed a little less defensive, "I'm sure you didn't. Paul's just looked at her and suggested I move her into the stable, she won't hear her pups crying for her from there. I've prepared a quiet corner for her that's why I've been so long. I'm sorry I won't be able to run you to the ferry terminal after all, I've got ten pups to look after for the next forty-eight hours. I'll just get Susie settled then I'll phone for a taxi, the telephone engineers have just repaired our line." As he spoke the words, Seb ran a frustrated hand through his hair, now he would have to let her go, pity, he was sure he could convince her that she didn't really love Alex.

Kim looked at him, he looked tired, and she knew she'd been the cause of his lost sleep. Now through no fault of his own, he wouldn't get much sleep for the next two nights!

Her heart softened, "Have you got anyone to help you with the pups?"

"Not at night no! My employee's go home to their families, accept for an elderly butler who lives in a flat in the east wing, and he's away visiting his daughter. The young maid Elsa only does three mornings to help my cook." He shot her a forlorn look as he scooped the dog up in his powerful arms and muttered a curse as he dropped a blanket.

Without another word she bundled up the clean blanket and followed him to the stable.

"Her bed is over there, if you could put the blanket in it," he asked breathing a little heavy from the exertion.
Kim did his bidding then watched as he lowered the dog down gently and soothed her with his large hand, speaking in that strange language he'd used when he'd calmed the horse last night. Kim had never seen anything like it, the dog lay down, and if she wasn't mistaken it was almost asleep.
"She's asleep!" she told him unnecessarily.
"Paul gave her something to calm her," he answered dismissively walking away from the big sleeping dog, "She'll be out for hours, I'll go and make up the pups feed, if you'll follow me we'll order a taxi for you."
He moved with an easy male gait ahead of her as they made their way back to the house. Kim had to walk briskly to keep up with the big man and by the look on his face, as he held the door open for her, he knew!
"My study is through there, the phone is on the desk," he indicated to a door leading off the kitchen. "You'll find the phone book in the right-hand drawer of my desk."
"Thanks," she replied a little breathlessly, more from his presence than from the brisk walk!

Witnessing the look of exhaustion in his eyes was her downfall. As soon as the thought came into her mind she regretted it, but her hand still returned the receiver to its cradle. 'It's madness, you're inviting trouble for yourself, the last place you want to be is in the company of this man! You're bound to give yourself away!' she argued with the small voice of conscience within her. 'It will mean staying by his side for forty-eight hours at least!' she warned, her conscience got the better of her. "You're a fool!" she muttered under her breath as she shut the desk drawer and made her way back to the kitchen, experience told her they would have to feed the newly born puppies every two to three hours, that was the best job. They would have to keep a constant check on their temperatures; newly born pups were susceptible to heat and cold. Not to mention the messy side of things, without the puppies' mother to help, they would have to stimulate them to get rid of their waste food. There will be little sleep for either of them!

Returning to the kitchen moments later, her mind firmly made up, she smiled at the sight that met her and knew she had made the right decision.
Seb had his back towards her and was pouring a milk solution into a row

of small bottles lined up along the worktop, and his language wasn't fit for any lady to hear. She nearly laughed out loud when one of the small bottles toppled spilling its contents, there was powder and milk splattered everywhere, so the big man wasn't always in control! Somehow his vulnerability touched her compassionate heart.

Sauntering up to the kitchen sink she rolled back her sleeves and washed her hands. Seb was so engrossed in the task at hand he hadn't noticed her reappearance. After drying her hands on a paper towel she stood next to him and started putting the teats on the bottles.
"Thanks," he muttered. "Have you booked your taxi?"
"No."
"Why not, you found the phone didn't you, or wasn't the book where I said it was?"
"I'll stay for a couple of days and help you feed the puppies!"
Seb stopped in his tracks and stared down at her. "What?"
"I said I'll help you feed the pups," she repeated hating herself for saying it, willing him to say he didn't want her to stay, but he didn't.
"Why?" he queried, trying hard to contain the look of triumph from showing on his face.
Kim shrugged, "I like puppies."
"And..." he asked, his golden eyes piercing into hers.
"And nothing," she answered feeling herself blushing at his scrutiny, she lowered her thick lashes and concentrated on the task before her. This was dangerous, she was very attracted to him. "There!" she said putting the last teat on the bottles.
"Give me a reason, why are you offering to help?"
Stealing a look at him she saw disbelief in his eyes, "Why should there be a reason, just take me up on the offer!" 'Why was she pleading with him to allow her to help!' she asked herself more bewildered by her offer than he was.
"If you're hoping to see Alex then you're wasting your time, he won't be back until next week."
"I'm aware of that and the thought never entered my mind."
"Then..."
"Look if you must know, I feel I owe you a favour."
"Favour?"
"Okay, I feel guilty, you lost two nights sleep because of me."
"I can't argue with that," he stated arrogantly, a glimmer of a smile tugging at the corners of his sensual mouth as he put the bottles onto a tray. "Come on it's going to be a long night!"

5

"Oh they're adorable!" she whispered. Seb had taken her into a large warm laundry room off the kitchen where Susie had chosen to have her pups. The puppies were in a large whelping box filled with paper. Kim's expert eyes assessed their health as she watched them, squeaking and writhing, blindly seeking their mother for food and warmth. "They seem extremely well, except for that one," she commented, pointing to a small bundle. It was smaller and shivering uncontrollably, the others were already pushing it away. After settling herself down on a blanket on the floor making sure her legs were tucked behind her, Kim reached in and lifted the tiny creature up and took a bottle from the tray. "You poor little thing," Kim whispered as it hooked hungrily onto the bottle.
"There's always a runt," Seb spoke softly sitting himself down on the floor next to her. "I don't think he'll make it, despite the heated box, he doesn't seem to be able to keep warm, I've named him Tiny Tim."
"Good job I'm here then!" she spoke without thinking.
Seb noted her comment. "You think so?"
"I-I just meant that if there are two of us looking after him he'll stand more of a chance!"
"Hmm." Seb answered unconvincingly.

An hour later all the puppies were sleeping, between them they had fed and done all they had to do for them, and all the time Kim kept Tiny Tim wrapped in a blanket on her knee, only putting him back when the others were asleep.
"I don't suppose you have got a hot water bottle?" she asked picking up the tray with the empty bottles on.
"I have, why do you ask?"

"I need it for Tiny Tim."
Seb nodded but warned, "Don't get too attached, I doubt he'll make it."
"Let me try, I've had experience of pulling sick pups through. If he doesn't it won't be because we didn't try," she whispered emotionally.
He followed her out to the kitchen his eyes taking in her beauty. "Okay," he agreed shaken by her show of compassion for a sick puppy.

After they had eaten a supper of sandwiches and cake, Seb left Kim washing and sterilising the bottles for the next feed,while he sorted out sleeping bags and camp beds for them to sleep on. She hummed a tune while she mixed up the formula for the night feeds and made flasks of coffee. She was just putting the feeds in the fridge when Seb returned with three hot water bottles. "I'll show you to your room if you're ready?"
"But I thought... we need to be near the puppies?"
"Yes of course but you'll need somewhere to change, may I suggest you wear jeans and a jumper if you have any. The nights are still a little cold," he stated stiffly as he gazed meaningfully at her short skirt, there was no mistaking the censure in his tawny eyes.
"Sure," Kim muttered pulling self-consciously at the offending clothing as she followed him into a large hall and up an elegant staircase, 'consider yourself chastised for not dressing more modestly!' she told herself with a smile as memories of her convent schooldays came flooding back.

Kim frowned as she pulled a thick jumper over her head, her thoughts reeling. Seb had left her at the top of the staircase, she sensed a sudden reluctance in him to escort her any further, was he afraid of her or his own feelings?
"Your room is the third door on the left," he had informed her abruptly, "If you'll excuse me I need to feed Susie and see to my other animals."
"Can I help?"
"No!" he snapped.
With that Kim found herself alone.
"I suppose it's asking for trouble entering a bedroom with a lady especially a lady with your morals! Why I might have molested him!" she told her reflection in a long mirror. 'And well you might have!' a small voice answered her back accusingly. Blushing she left the room and returned to the kitchen.

Seb had changed from the milk splattered business suit he was wearing earlier into blue jeans and a sweater. Kim stood gazing at the entrance of the kitchen absolutely spellbound, totally unable to take her eyes off him. She took in his dark handsome features and big powerful

body, watching his muscles ripple across his back as he made up a camp bed in front of the big Aga cooker. A tremble shook her body and an ache started in her inner core for reasons she didn't want to admit to. Suddenly sensing her presence he turned around giving her a smouldering look of disdain that told her he knew what she was thinking before he lowered his thick lashes! Kim sucked in her breath, he had actually blushed. Mortified and more than a little embarrassed that he had caught her watching him she quickly looked away, lest he saw the wanting, but she had a feeling it was too late.
"You are sleeping in here, I've made my bed up in there," he muttered curtly pointing to the room where the puppies were.
"F-fine, how is Susie?"
"I've given her another tablet, she was a little fractious, she's sleeping now and I suggest we do the same. We have," he clipped, pulling back his jumper and looking at his watch, "just under two hours. I suggest we feed them then, and try to get a nap ourselves in between."
"I would like to see to Tiny Tim first."

Not waiting for him to agree she filled the hot water bottles he'd left on the kitchen table and strode into the laundry room with a fluffy towel tucked under her arm, glad of an excuse to get away from him. Peering into the whelping box she tutted, the little animal was starting to shiver again, puppies were like babies they needed to be kept warm. Picking him up gently she wrapped the tiny creature loosely in the towel igloo fashion and returned him to the box tucking the warm bottles against the towel.
She jumped as Seb leaned over her shoulder, his breath fanned her cheeks. "Any chance of me getting any sleep tonight!" he hissed in her ear.
"Sure, don't mind me, he's stopped shivering and he's almost asleep!" she answered breathlessly.
"Perhaps you should sleep here and I'll sleep in the kitchen!" he muttered irritably.
"I would prefer to, I really do need to keep an eye on Tiny Tim!" she whispered back flashing him a charming smile in an effort to defuse the tension between them, it was his turn to suck in his breath. "Sleep well!" She nearly giggled as he muttered an answer under his breath and strode out of the room closing the door firmly, judging by his behaviour, she wasn't the only one effected by this chemistry that had risen up between them!

Satisfied that Tiny was warmer she pulled the camp bed closer to the whelping box and crawled gratefully under the duvet. Sighing blissfully as her head sank into the pillow she shut her eyes it was only nine o'clock in the evening but not surprisingly sleep soon claimed her.

She awoke to the sound of whimpering puppies, groaning she staggered into the kitchen. Seb was mixing something into the feeds she had made up earlier, silently she stood by his side and helped. "I've added a supplement that Paul left to this feed so with a bit of luck we may have three hours sleep!"
"Heaven!" Kim answered as she padded bare foot behind him.

Again she lifted the smallest puppy out and fed him, she didn't want him to get too hungry, he might choke if he tried to gulp it down too quick. "He really does need his mother's milk," Kim commented.
"Well there is nothing I can do about that!" he answered sternly.
Kim grimaced and kept silent, it obviously suited the man. The only word he uttered was a clipped 'good night' when they'd finished.
Kim childishly stuck her tongue out at his retreating figure, "miserable ungrateful man!" she muttered very quietly to herself.
To her consternation he came back into the room his eyes pierced into hers. "I'm not miserable or ungrateful! I'm just tired, forgive me." With that he left.
Kim blushed and her mouth dropped open, 'how had he heard that?' she wondered remembering again what Alex had said.

"Fiona! Wake up!"
"W-what, go away!" she groaned, feeling aggrieved with the person shaking her awake.
"Fiona, the puppies need feeding!" a voice intruded.
Kim sat up and rubbed her eyes, grimacing as Seb turned the dimmer switch up. "Oh what I wouldn't give to turn over and go back to sleep!" she muttered pushing the duvet away and swinging her long jean clad legs onto the floor and pushing her feet into her slippers.
"You and me both!" he agreed. "If you've changed your mind, you know where your bed is upstairs."
"I haven't changed my mind," she yawned sleepily taking a bottle from the tray and sitting on the floor next to Seb. "What time is it?"
"Three o'clock," he answered curtly, shuffling a few inches away from her as his eyes took in her flushed sleepy face, she really was temptation with a capital 'T'.
Kim noticed his evasive action and clicked her tongue as she picked up a whimpering puppy and started feeding it. "I think you're so cute," she

told it drowsily laughing at the little creature's eagerness to suckle.
"I wonder if you'll think he's so cute after forty-eight hours of non stop feeding and nursing?"
Seb retorted dryly.

Between them they fed all the puppies in half an hour. Tiny Tim managed to take all of his milk. Seb refilled the hot water bottles while she settled him into his 'igloo' again.
"Coffee?" Seb asked picking up one of the flasks.
Kim nodded and gratefully took the cup of steaming hot liquid from him making sure her hands didn't touch his, "Thanks."
He grunted a reply. They drank in silence, not wanting to disturb the puppies who were sleeping contentedly again.
Seb took her empty cup from her, "Get back to bed, I'll wake you for the next feed." With that he left shutting the door firmly behind him. Kim shrugged at his coldness as she returned to her camp bed, she would look forward to the day when he knew the truth about her.

Sunlight was filtering through a gap in the curtains when Kim opened her eyes. Glancing at her watch she noticed it was almost five, the puppies were beginning to stir for their next feed. In an effort to wake herself up she splashed her face with cold water from the utility sink before opening the door to the kitchen.
Seb glanced over his shoulder when she entered the room his searching eyes swept briefly over her curvaceous figure. "Good, you're up," he stated putting the teats on the bottles of feed. "I was just about to wake you."
"The puppies whimpering woke me."
"Let's get to it!" he smiled. "Then you can make us a bacon sandwich while I make the coffee."
"It's a deal," she agreed amazed at his sudden change of mood.

Tiny Tim was fed first, "How is he this morning?" Seb asked watching intently as she encouraged the little creature to finish the bottle.
"He managed to right himself when he fell over one of the others and he's not shivering. He would benefit from his mother's milk and an incubator, I'd like to weigh him, what did he weighed at birth?"
"I can't remember exactly, the papers are on my desk in the study, perhaps you would like to have a look at them after breakfast?"

While Kim grilled the bacon, Seb put the coffee machine on, and opened the back door; he stood filling his lungs with the fresh morning

air. "It's a beautiful day!" he exclaimed stretching his long frame feeling self-righteous with himself, he'd made it through the night with this temptress.
Kim glanced up taking in the wonderful sea view from the open door, the birds were singing and, although it was only six o'clock, the sun was casting long shadows on the dew soaked grass, making it sparkle like thousands of diamonds.
"You have a wonderful home," she spoke quietly coming to stand beside him breathing in the delicate perfume of the blossoming trees, "it's so peaceful."
"I think so, I shall miss it when Alex takes over," he agreed his eyes looking up at the clouds as they moved across the azure sky like fluffy sheep.
"Is that your intention?" she asked, "to hand it over to Alex?"
For a moment he frowned, and she thought he wasn't going to answer her.
"I want to pursue my own vocation," he stated flatly rubbing at the seven o'clock blue black shadow on his face. "Is that my bacon burning woman?"

He laughed as she ran screeching towards the grill, "I know you like me, but I didn't expect burnt offerings so soon."
"I haven't burnt it!" she cried indignantly feeling herself blush from head to foot, had he guessed how she felt about him? She must try to hide the feelings that he managed to inflict on her, especially as he had just told her he was going back to the ministry. Her happy mood popped like a burst bubble as she thought over his words, leaving her in a pensive mood. "Breakfast is ready, and I wouldn't stand in the strong sunlight too long, you might crumble away into a pile of dust."
Missing her sad mood, Seb grinned to himself, 'heavens did he really look that evil?' He wandered back into the room and poured out the coffees, "Remarks like that could give a guy a complex!"
"Not you, you're too arrogant!"
"Maybe!" he laughed. "But to be likened to Count Dracula is hitting below the belt!"
"Then I won't tease you anymore."
His long hand reached out and cupped her chin, lifting her face to look at him. "Is that what you were doing, teasing me?"
"Possibly," she stated shyly pulling away from his hold and handing him his sandwich.

They sat and ate in an amiable silence, each lost in their own thoughts.

"We'll wash the bottles and the breakfast things, then you check over the puppies details while I do my work and check on Susie, that's if you want, you may want to get some sleep?" Seb said after they had eaten.

Kim looked at the strong handwriting on the forms before her with admiration, Seb was very efficient, noting all the information that the kennel club would need to know.
She was halfway through when the phone rang. "Seb?" she called walking over to the door. "Seb, telephone!"
The kitchen was empty; he must still be with Susie. The phone continued to ring, she would have to answer it.
"Hello Sir Worsley's residence."
"Who's that?" a confused voice answered.
"Um...Sir Worsley's not here at the moment can I take a message and get him to phone you back?"
"Kim! Is that you?"
"Alex?"
"Yes, what are you doing there?" he inquired.
"Helping Seb with Susie's pups, she developed a milk infection so between us we are feeding them."
His voice faltered, "He knows you are not Fiona then?"
"No, he still doesn't know," she reassured. "Is Fiona there?"
"Right beside me," he answered the relief evident. "Shall I pass her on."
"Please do!"
"Kim, it's me!" her sister's bright voice came down the line.
"Never mind 'it's me,' I'm really angry with you."
"Why?" her twin answered.
"You have the nerve to ask that? I'm angry because you've gone to Scotland and left me here to finish the holiday on my own after persuading me to come away with you, and do you realise you have the car keys!" she added for good measure.
"Oh Kim, I'm so sorry I didn't realise, I'll post them on. What are you doing at the Manor?"
"I had little choice, you left with the car keys and the telephone lines were down after the storm. Seb didn't want to leave me there without any means of contact, he said it was too cut off."
"I've said I'm sorry, look we'll both be home at the week-end, stay at the Manor until then, please it's important, and I promise you we will tell Seb the truth."
"I don't know I..."
"Please Kim I need you to...I really am sorry but you'll realise why in three days time...Look Alex is getting impatient, I've got to go, I love

you, I don't suppose you love me anymore?" she asked wretchedly.
Hearing the remorse in her sister's voice, as always Kim softened, "Of course I still love you, but I'm very cross. You should not have left me here..."
Seb's polite cough let her know he had come into the office.
Sucking in her breath in surprise she spoke quickly into the receiver, "Seb has returned I'll pass you on to him."
"I'll pass Alex on, love you..." Fiona muttered.

Freshly shaved, his hair still wet from a shower Seb took the receiver from her hand and cast her a scowl, the amicable mood had burst. "I'll go and weigh Tiny..." she mumbled as she retreated out of his office. How much of the conversation had he heard, had she given the game away by speaking Fiona's name? 'Too late now,' she told herself groaning as she went over and over the conversation, she was sure she hadn't.

Picking up Tiny Tim she put him on the scales. "Good, it's not a lot, but at least you've put some weight on, keep it up little one," she told the small creature before she put him back into his warm igloo. She felt his presence even before she turned around as it penetrated to her very soul, stirring her senses.
"So you've persuaded him to come home for the weekend?" he grated.
"Pardon?"
"Don't prevaricate Fiona, you know he's coming home this week-end, he's asked me to keep you here until then."
"Oh!" was all she could reply.
"If I had my way, you would be on the next ferry home!"
"I didn't persuade him."
"He will return on Monday Fiona, is that clear?" he asked crossly, ignoring her denial.
"Please don't be angry, you don't understand..."
"Too right I don't," he rasped.
Kim didn't answer, she heard him swear under his breath, "I'm taking Susie with me to see Paul, I'll be back this afternoon."
Shutting her eyes tight to stop the sudden sting of tears she managed a nod.
"I've roped Joan, my cook, and a few others into helping with the daytime feeds while I'm away, feel free to do and use whatever you want. I advise you to get some rest too."
His words came with ice and she flinched as the door closed, he hadn't slammed it, but all the same it jarred her. It shocked her that the man had the power to hurt, but hurt her he had. There was a dull ache in her chest

and a lone tear trickled its way down her cheek, she brushed it away irritably. 'Why are you so hurt, what could he possibly mean to you?' she asked herself. 'You're in love with him!' came a mocking voice from within.
"Stupid woman, you don't know him," she admonished herself, why, hadn't she told Fiona only last year that love at first sight just didn't happen, it was sexual attraction and chemistry that's all! The sooner she got away from him and this place the better, 'The feelings would soon disappear,' she assured herself. As soon as Susie could feed her pups again, she would leave, there was no way she was going to wait for Fiona and Alex to return from Scotland.

6

It was early afternoon and Seb still hadn't returned to the house, Joan had helped with the morning feeds. Stiff and achy, Kim ate a sandwich then decided to go for a short walk around the Manor House to stretch her legs. Curiosity led her to look for the 'farm zoo' he had spoken about in the pub yesterday. Yesterday! Was it only yesterday, to Kim it seemed like a lifetime ago?
A young stable lad was just taking a pony into the stables as she approached and she asked him to show her where the collection of animals was kept.
"You must be Fiona, Master Seb said you would probably be along to see them," the young lad grinned cheekily as if he was sharing a joke with 'the master.'
"Well he wasn't wrong then was he?" she answered regretting asking.
"Master Seb is never wrong, he said you knew a lot about animals, I'm nearly finished here, give me a moment to put her away then I'll take you to them."
"Thanks," she said smiling back, there was little point in being annoyed with him.

Seb's 'farm zoo' was made up of about fifty different animals, both wild and domesticated. According to the stable boy Darren, some of the wild animals had been abandoned by their mothers at birth, and were hand reared by Seb or Darren. Others had injuries that made it impossible for them to be released back into the wild. A lucky few had recovered and were waiting to be released.
"I'll show you the hospital, that's where we treat the injured," Darren informed her.
The extensive medical room impressed Kim, it was well equipped to

handle most emergency treatments.
"This is our latest casualty," Darren said as he led her over to one of the large cages. "The police found him lying in the road, he was hit by a car. Legs broken, but it is mending nicely, we'll be releasing him soon."
Kim looked at the badger, "Poor thing, he's not very old!"
"No, vet said he's about a year, that's all."
"He's lucky that you have this place."
The boy nodded, "It's pretty quiet at the moment, though with lambing season starting, it will soon be full of lambs."
"How come?"
"Master Seb has an agreement with the neighbouring farmers, they allow him to have a few sheep and their newly born lambs for a week, children come from the local schools to see the lambs with their mothers..." Darren stopped mid-sentence a frown marring his young face as he looked over Kim's shoulder. "Oh no, now what?"
Kim spun around and watched as a police car approached them.
"Another patient, I'm afraid," a policeman called over to them as he got out of the car.
Kim pushed her hands into her jacket pockets and walked over to the officer with Darren. "Sir Worsley's out for the morning, is it serious?" Darren asked.
"Young fox, some youngsters found him in a field caught up in some wire, they managed to free the wire from the fence but it's still wrapped around the fox." The officer's partner opened the back door of the car and took out an animal wrapped in a blanket. "He's unconscious."
Darren led them into the hospital.
Kim followed firing orders at Darren. "Put him on the table, get me a syringe with Domitor, lets keep him subdued, I don't want him coming round just yet for all our sakes."
Darren didn't question, he handed her the sedative, and watched as she cut the wire off the fox.
"It's a snare," she muttered crossly, "trouble is the more they struggle the tighter the snare gets. He's got a nasty slash on his back, I'll need to stitch it, get me the suturing kit...and the antibiotics."

Kim worked quickly on the animal watched by the police and Darren. "There," she said as she stood back, "put him into the cage and cover it, he'll feel more secure in the dark. Poor thing must have got exhausted in his struggle to free himself, hopefully he'll be fine after a few days rest."

Darren saw the police back to their car while Kim put all the medicines back into the cabinets and disposed of the syringe safely.

"That was marvellous what you did," Darren said when he returned. "Master Seb said you were a veterinary nurse."
"Thanks," she muttered grateful that the injury wasn't more serious, what she had just done was well within the capabilities of any good veterinary nurse. If it had been more serious she would have treated the animal, she had no option, but she'd have a lot of explaining to do to Seb.
After checking that all the medicines cabinets were locked, Darren smiled and made his way over to the door, "Well I suppose I must get on, if you'll excuse me, I've got to muck out the pigs before Master Seb returns."
"Of course, thanks for your assistance," Kim replied, returning his smile.
"My pleasure, bye now."

Kim walked quickly back to the house, the puppies were due for another feed. As she walked into the kitchen Joan told her Seb had phoned.
"He has gone onto an urgent meeting. The vet said Susie is fine and the pups can start feeding from her tomorrow morning. He also wanted me to tell you to have a break, I told him you hadn't rested this morning. Why don't you have a nap, my lad Mark is on his way, he'd be disappointed if he couldn't help feed them, he's helped Seb feed different animals that have come here before. Seb's giving him one of the pups for his birthday.
"Giving?" Kim queried.
"Yes, he really is the kindest man I have ever known, apart from my Bert that is!" she amended. "Now off you go, you look all in."
Kim agreed, "Okay, I could do with a soak in the bath and a change of clothes," she conceded gratefully rubbing her aching neck, "but you will wake me if you feel Tiny is in any trouble won't you?"
"I promise," Joan answered.

Kim was horrified when she woke up and looked at the small brass clock on the bedside table, "Oh no it can't be!" she cried. It was eight o'clock, she'd slept for almost seven hours!
Quickly splashing water on her face and brushing her tousled hair, she ran down stairs into the kitchen.
"Ah there you are, I was just going to come up and wake you. Mark helped me feed the puppies half an hour ago before he went on to youth group, so you can sit down and have your meal in peace, Seb made up the feeds with the supplement so they should go three hours. If you're ready

I'll dish your dinner up for you, sit down," Joan said smiling indicating that Kim took the place laid for her at the kitchen table. "You look much better."
"I feel it, the bath must have made me sleepy, you should have woken me, I didn't mean to sleep that long."
Joan took a plate out of the Aga and put in on the table in front of her, "Master Seb told us not to wake you."
"He's back, where is he?" Kim asked sniffing appreciatively at the delicious casserole Joan had set before her.
"He returned with Susie at about six, settled her into the stable then, after making up the feeds, had his meal with my Bert. They'd just finished when the phone rang, poor man had to go out again, said he'd be back before the next feed."
The sound of a car horn turned Joan's attention to the window, "That'll be my Bert," she said taking off her apron, "have you everything you need?"
"Yes, you go and thank you for feeding the pups."
"It was a pleasure," Joan grinned shrugging into her coat, "I'll see you tomorrow."

Joan shut the back door after her and a hush fell in the big old house, interrupted only by the loud ticking of the grandfather clock in the hall. For the want of something to do, Kim went into Seb's office and finished reading the reports for the kennel club. She stayed there until it was time to get the feeds ready. Looking at her watch she sighed, surely Seb would be back soon, it was gone eleven!

When the puppies began to stir she decided to start. "Oh well looks like I'm on my own!" she muttered carrying the bottles through into the room where the pups where. Sitting on her camp bed she picked up the puppy nearest to her and started feeding. It took her almost an hour to feed and see to all their needs. After tucking Tiny into his igloo with his warm bottles, she returned to the kitchen. It was then that her eyes caught the tin of dog food, "Oh my goodness, Susie!" The poor dog hadn't had her evening meal and if she was going to start feeding her puppies again tomorrow it was imperative that she ate tonight.

Zipping her fleece up to her chin she picked up the dog's things and dropping them into a bag headed towards the stable. Feeling more worried than annoyed with Seb, she began to wonder if he was alright? Kim tutted and pulled herself up, 'if he weren't someone would have informed you by now!' she thought opening the stable door and switching the lights on before shutting it firmly behind her and let out a squeal of terror as she faced the ferocious dog.

How she managed to dive so quickly into the nearest stall and shut the slatted gate after her, she would never know. Her heart was pounding and she was trembling with fear. Pressing herself flat against the wall, keeping well away from the big horse's hoofs, she tried to speak calmly to the snarling barking animal, if she could calm Susie the horse would settle. "Susie! Shh. It's me." The dog growled and, pulling back her snout, bared her big teeth at her. If she could reach the bag that she'd dropped, she could distract Susie with the food and make her escape.
She waited until Susie stopped barking, then edging her way slowly around the stall a small step at a time until she was within inches of the bag, talking quietly to the agitated horse, she tried to reach for it. Susie was one step ahead and Kim withdrew her hand inside the bars as the dog snapped at her hand. "Damn," she swore, the bag was just out of her reach. 'Of all the stupid situations to be in!' she chided herself. Susie was a guard dog and she was protecting her master's property! There was nothing she could do but wait for someone to come and rescue her. Shutting her eyes her heart sank as she groaned in frustration, "And I can just about guess who that person will be!"

Half an hour later Susie had taken guard by the pen, although she was laying down in the straw seemingly asleep, Kim had no pretensions as to the dog's capability to spring into action at her slightest move from her protective jail. If only she could reach the food! Looking around she saw a riding crop hung up on a hook, if she stood on tiptoe she might be able to reach then she could use it to drag the bag nearer to her! With one eye on the sleeping dog she edged her way along the wall, holding her breath and stopping when she saw the creature stir. "Phew!" she muttered continuing to move when the dog settled again. Her fingers had just wrapped around the crop when the door opened wide, sucking in her breath she turned to see Seb, the crop fell from her hand.

Quickly assessing the situation, Seb called the dog over to him and, catching her by the collar, patted her before he put a lead on. Talking reassuring to the dog he led her into a small room off the main stable and shut her in.
As it was now safe Kim opened the barrier and sauntered out, brushing herself down, looking more confident than she felt, she watched him advance towards her with a terrifying look of anger on his handsome face.
She gulped as he stood in front of her, his golden eyes glittering with

rage. 'Stand up to him,' she advised herself, 'it was his fault for leaving you here alone, remember what your daddy told you, attack is the best form of defence.' Taking a deep breath she spoke sternly at him, "Where the hell have you been?"
She squealed as he grabbed hold of her upper arms almost lifting her feet off the ground and shook her unmercifully. "You bloody fool, don't you know she's a guard dog?" he spat out.
Digging her nails into her palms to stop a nervous giggle from escaping, she muttered whimsically. "The thought had occurred to me."
Pulling her so close that his face was only inches away, his nostrils flaring, he gave her another shake, "Woman don't be flippant with me, the animal could have killed you!"
"Susie wouldn't have killed me, not if you've trained her right!"
"I'm not talking about Susie, she was happy to keep you pinned to the wall, I was talking about Black Fury, you could have been kicked to death!" he hollered back.

As his words sank in Kim cast a sideways look at the narrow stall she'd ran into and gulped, he was right, if the big horse had been skittish she wouldn't have stood a chance! Anger welled up inside, he'd put her in this position, it was his fault! "If you had come back earlier this wouldn't have happened, I saw Susie's food in the kitchen, after I'd fed the puppies on my own. I-I came here to f-feed her..." her voice cracked as she tried to blink back the sudden rush of tears as the enormity of the situation hit her.

Seeing her tears and shocked white face Seb's fury melted in seconds, wrapping his arms around her he pulled her gently close, "Shhh," he whispered. "Don't cry, I didn't mean to shout at you, its just reaction to what could have happened to you."

Touched by his sudden gentleness Kim wrapped her arms around his slim waist and laying her head on his big chest, let the tears fall.
"Hey, hey come on," he said gently putting his hands either side of her cheeks and lifting her face so that he could see her. His thumbs started wiping the tears away, "It's been a terrible ordeal, and I'm sorry I yelled at you, forgive me?" Bending down, his mouth kissed her salty cheeks.

7

Whether he turned his face or she did, Kim wasn't sure, she heard herself whisper his name before he lowered his mouth on hers. She felt an ache deep inside as she moved nearer to him. His seductive groan heightened her hunger and her lips parted greeting the moist assault of his tongue. His hands slowly wandered lower down her back and propelled her hips against his, leaving her in no doubt that he desired her. Her loins melted as she willingly moulded her yielding body against his, transcending everything but the need to give her all to this formidable sexy man.

Suddenly Seb growled and pulled abruptly away, holding her at arm length with one hand, "No!" he uttered shaking his head, his voice dark with passion, his other hand grasping the large silver cross he wore around his neck, his fingers curling around it. "I-I can't...my vow...and you..." he snarled with utter contempt, his breath laboured, his eyes dazed and heavy with carnality, "you ...are supposed to be in love with my brother, or have you forgotten him so quickly!"

With a sob that shook her whole being, unable to stand the look of loathing on his face for another moment, Kim shook his restraining hand away and ran from the stable.

Stumbling blindly she ran back to the house, going straight up to her room and into the en-suite, she splashed her burning hot face with cold water. Picking up the fluffy towel she buried her head into it, 'What have I done?' she asked herself. 'Driven a holy man into temptation,' she answered ashamedly. How could she face him again, not only did he think she was two-timing his brother, he also thought she was a harlot?

It was an hour later when she made the decision that it was better to face him now, rather than wait until later, anyway the pup's next feed was due soon and the bottles needed to be made up, her professional side kicked in. Embarrassed, she slowly made her way downstairs, she would apologise to Seb and assure him the incident only happened because of the fraught situation she was in, hopefully that would be an end to the incident. After all it was only a kiss for heavens sake! She groaned as she remembered the kiss, 'only' wasn't an apt description!

The kitchen was empty so she went through to the laundry room and checked on the puppies. They were sleeping. Going back into the kitchen she started making the feeds.
By the time she had finished her task, Seb hadn't returned, she could hear the puppies stirring, 'Still sulking in the stable, hopefully suffering from a guilty conscience,' she thought more than a little piqued, 'trying to think up some appropriate act of contrition for both of them for committing such wicked behaviour!'

Seb's absence caused her relief, despite her earlier conviction that it was better to face him! Missing her bed wasn't a problem, she doubted whether she would be able to sleep anyway. The next and last feed was due at dawn and if she packed her things straight after she had finished this feed, she wouldn't have to talk to the man ever again. That thought should have made her feel happier, but it didn't. She fed Tiny first, or tried to, he was extremely lethargic and didn't want to take the milk.
"I'll leave you until last," she told him as she settled him lovingly back into his warm cocoon.

With all the others fed she picked Tiny up again, he was worse. In fact he was failing and failing fast. It was the last straw; unable to keep the deluge back she gave way to heartbreaking sobs.
"Fiona?" he inquired softly as he walked into the room. "Don't cry, for the second time this night I apologise for my inappropriate behaviour, I was grossly out of order. I...oh no!" he stated as he saw the listless puppy. "Give him to me," he demanded.
Kim tearfully handed him over, "He's not taken his food."
Ignoring her he said, "Earlier this evening I went to see a friend, her dog gave birth to one puppy, it died, that's why I was so late, it took time to persuade her. I've brought the dog back with me, the dog's got enough milk for Tiny, I'm just not sure whether she'll allow Tiny to suckle."
"Where is she?" Kim leapt up, hope sparkling in her over moist eyes.
"In the lounge, I... "
"Bring Tiny," she ordered, picking up a piece of clean towelling.

Seb grinned as he watched her retreating, it looked like he'd managed to get one thing right tonight. Getting up he followed her into the lounge carrying the puppy with care.

Kim sat down on the floor next to the box containing a Golden Labrador. "Hi there, what's your name?" she asked the dog in a whisper, stroking her soft fur with the piece of towelling, all her problems with Seb pushed to the back of her mind as she concentrated on saving Tiny.
"Goldie," Seb's deep voice rumbled behind her.
"Hello Goldie," Kim spoke softly to the dog and continued to stroke her, then taking the cloth with the scent of Goldie, she wrapped it around Tiny Tim's small body, and gently talking in a reassuring voice to the Labrador, inched Tiny nearer.

Seb watched amazed as she introduced the small puppy and breathed a sigh of relief when the mother dog licked the little one and allowed it to suckle.
"Whatever possessed you to give up working with animals, you're a natural!" he commented gruffly.
Hoping a shrug would deter any further questions, she moved slowly away from the whelping box.

The change in the small creature's health was almost immediate as it buried itself against the larger dog, she smiled as it sucked noisily from its new mother.
"Tiny should pull through, he obviously needed natural milk!" Kim said wiping away a tear, "Thank you."
He nodded, unable to answer her, she was so beautiful she took his breath away, and if he didn't distance himself from her, he couldn't be responsible for what happened. Yesterday he thought he could handle it, come on to her to prove that she didn't love Alex! But today the tables had turned, for the first time in years his desire for a woman had returned, his whole body ached to hold her again, trust him to pick the one he could never have to thaw his frozen heart!
"You better get some rest, I'll sit up with Tiny, I'll sleep on the sofa," he ordered.
"I'd like to stay..."
"I think not, go to bed Fiona, for both our sakes!"
She resisted the urge to slam the door, at least he's admitted the fault wasn't entirely hers.

Back in her room, knowing sleep wasn't an option, she packed the few things she'd unpacked on her arrival. After closing the case she dragged it over to the door ready for Seb to take downstairs for her. Glancing at the clock she sighed, it was three o'clock and she was wide-awake! 'Get some rest,' an inner voice advised her, taking heed she lay on top of the covers and waited for dawn to shed its watery light.

It was almost six o'clock when she crept silently down the stairs past the lounge door and into the kitchen.
"Fiona?"
"Why do you always do that to me?" she asked crossly, jumping with fright.
"Do what?" he asked a glimmer of a smile pulling at the corner of his lips.
"Creep up on me!"
"Sorry, I heard you coming down the stairs, but I didn't call out, I want you to take a look at Tiny," he said his face taking on a stern look.
"Is he worse?" she asked with trepidation.
"Come and see for yourself."
He was already halfway down the hall, so she had little option but to follow.
He held the lounge door open for her.

Sucking in her breath she looked into the box, "Oh Tiny, just look at you."
"Isn't it great!" Seb whispered behind her.
She nodded, too full up to answer as she watched the surrogate mother cleaning a very lively little puppy, who like any little boy wasn't keen on having a wash.
"Thank you," she whispered back, "I owe you, will your friend allow you to keep her dog until Tiny is weaned?"
"Louise will do anything I ask of her, she is coming to stay for a few days so that she can be near Goldie," 'and act as chaperone!' he thought to himself.
Kim digested this information, he had spent all of yesterday evening with Louise, the nun in the photograph. A stab of jealousy wounded her heart, then anger took it's place, he had left her to feed the puppies on her own to be with another woman, then he'd come back shouted at her, kissed her, spoken of vows he'd made! 'Had he broken that vow earlier, what had he just said? "Louise will do anything I ask of her."' she wondered, feeling the knife twist inside her. Poor woman, Seb was the sort of man who could persuade a saint to sin.'
"Well come on, let's leave them we've one more feed to do, then I'll bring

Susie back and reacquaint her with her puppies."
Seething inside she followed him.

"I've decided to go home today," she stated when they were both sat in the kitchen eating their breakfast.
Seb put his teacup down in the saucer with a clatter, his hands not entirely steady, "You can't do that, Alex is coming home for the weekend!"
She shrugged, "He'll understand." 'And so will you by then,' she said to herself.
Anger flashed in his golden eyes, "I don't, Alex will want to know why you've left in such a hurry and if he asks, I'll tell him the truth. That will cause all sorts of problems, he would no longer want to work here, I couldn't follow my life's ambition and all because of a stupid kiss!"
'Ouch!' Kim thought as she noted the 'stupid'.
He had pushed his chair back and was pacing around the kitchen, "Don't do this to us Fiona, it has taken me years to make things up with Alex! Look please stay, it will only be for a few days."
"No, and you flatter yourself if you think I'm leaving because of what happened last night, as you so rightly said, it was just a stupid kiss."

For a moment there was absolute silence in the room, Kim watched his back straighten and waited for the explosion.
He came back to the table and putting both his hands down, leaned towards her his tawny eyes piecing into hers. "Paul gave me a list of dogs which had recently whelped when I saw him yesterday. I then spent all afternoon looking for a surrogate mother and an evening persuading my friend to part with her beloved dog, for a runt that you've got yourself attached to, and that's all the thanks I get!" he hissed. His shoulders suddenly slumped, as the anger dissipated, "Please Fiona, don't destroy the fragile relationship I have with my brother, he's all I've got now."
Seeing his torment, Kim lowered her gaze and gulped, she didn't want him worried, he didn't have to be, she wasn't Alex's woman. 'Tell him the truth!' an inner voice nagged. She sighed, by doing that before Alex could explain himself would destroy the relationship, she had little option but to stay, and he had saved Tiny she owed him that.
"Ok, I'll stay," she whispered.
"Thank you," he breathed out in relief, he didn't want to tell his brother what had happened between them, but most of all he didn't want her to go! 'God what a mess!'

With Susie happily reunited with her pups and Tiny Tim recovering fast with his new mother, Kim returned to her room to unpack once more.

She was just hanging a dress in the wardrobe when someone knocked on the door.
"Come in," she invited.
"The postman has just delivered a parcel for you Fiona, do you want a hand unpacking, I've finished all my chores for now?" Joan's happy smiling face peeped around the door.
"I've just finished thank you," she smiled back as she shut the wardrobe and wandered over to the cook.
"Well come and have a coffee, I'll bring it into the lounge for you."
"I'd rather have it in the kitchen with you," Kim replied with a smile as she took the small packet off her.
"I'll put the kettle on then, see you in a minute."

When Joan had gone, Kim looked at the handwriting on the parcel, it was from Fiona. Tearing it open she looked inside. "Wonderful," she cried as she shook the car keys out of the packet onto the bed cover, after coffee she would walk back to the cottage and pick the car up, maybe go for a drive this afternoon and tomorrow if the weather held. That way she would not have to stay in Seb's company and it would give her a chance to see some of this beautiful Island. Fiona and Alex would be back the following day then, after they had told 'his lordship' the truth she could drive back home on Saturday, in fact he'd probably send her packing. She couldn't imagine Seb being in a good mood when he found out he'd been duped by Alex.

After checking that the puppies were alright she had a pleasant chat over coffee with Joan, then set out to retrieve the car. It was another pleasant spring day. Joan had informed her that Seb would be gone all morning, and he was returning with his friend, Louise. She had chatted away at how she'd made up another guestroom, something she hadn't done since Lord William, Seb's father, passed away. So Seb was bringing Louise back with him today, he was probably with her now, a stab of pain shot through her. Thrusting her hands deep into her pockets she quickened her pace along the country lane, she had told Joan that the package she'd received contained a set of car keys for her car and she was going to explore the area so she would have her lunch and dinner out. She had every intention of staying away from the Manor House, she was regretting giving Seb the cottage keys back. Now she was mobile again and the phone lines were reconnected, there was no earthly reason for her to stay at the Manor House, in fact she would prefer not to, the thought of Seb and Louise together nearly tore her heart apart.

Kim returned to the cottage and stood looking at the logs piled neatly near where the old oak tree had stood only a few days ago. An old man was sweeping the pathway of debris and a large white van was parked in front of Fiona's car.
"Why have you cut it down?" she asked him walking over to him.
"Lightening struck it, it weren't safe, the middle was almost hollow!"
"That's a shame it was a lovely tree," Kim retorted.
"'Twas a shame, still, now we'll see if the legend comes true!"
The legend, Kim had forgotten about it, seeing her chance of finding out she questioned the man. "What legend?"

The old man grinned and lent on his broom handle, only too pleased to relate the tale. "Around the twelfth century, the Lord of Ashill returned from a pilgrimage to the Holy Land to find his home, Ashill Manor, taken over and his young pretty wife, Lady Rose, murdered in this very spot, by his uncle."
"Why did he murder her?" Kim shuddered.
"She refused his advances, so he banished her to a peasants cottage that stood on the very spot of that there cottage, hoping she would change her mind about him."
"Did she?"
"No, he was old and ugly, and she was madly in love with her husband, 'tis said the uncle murdered her the day before her husband came home."
"How awful."
"Aye, the husband found her body, he buried her right here!" he pointed to the stump of the oak. "And planted an acorn, promising that their love would go on, and both of them would return to Ashill Manor in another life, this would happen when the oak died. He regained his home, killed the wicked uncle but sadly died soon after of a broken heart."
"Really?" Kim laughed in disbelief. "Sounds like an adaptation of Robin Hood!"
"Don't you be mockin' stranger things happen on this Island and her ghost has been seen many a time around here and in the cottage!"
Kim pulled her face into a solemn mask, "So I've heard," she acknowledged as she opened Fiona's car door, feeling the temperature drop a few degrees, she shivered. "I hope I never meet her!"
"Me too, have a nice day," the man agreed throwing the broom into the back of his white van. "I'll move the van."

Luckily for Kim, Fiona had picked up some brochures of places of interest on the boat over and had put them in the glove compartment. After sorting through them, Kim decided that today she would try to see a few of the 'wonders' of the Isle of Wight. After studying a small map at the back of the brochure she discovered that the nearest to her were the Needles. Putting the papers back in the glove compartment she turned the key in the ignition, the engine fired first time. "Needles you can't thread, here we come," she stated as she put the car into gear and moved forward.

Soon she had joined the coastal 'Military Road' and headed west. The winding road climbed steeply, and the picturesque view took her breath away. Pulling into a parking area she stopped to take some photos. Her next 'wonder' was the town of Freshwater, there she bought some sandwiches and ate them in a small park before heading on to Yarmouth. When she pulled into Yarmouth anger and amazement shot through her when she realised that there was another ferry terminal. Seb could have easily driven her here and still had time to get to his meeting last Monday, so why hadn't he? Kim stiffened, was he keeping her here because he knew the truth, that she wasn't Fiona? Like on other occasions he had somehow known! The man was a complete mystery to her! Well she wasn't going to waste her time on trying to figure him out. Now she had the car keys back she was free, free to spend her time enjoying the Island. Pushing aside all her new emotions, Kim spent most of the afternoon wandering around the quaint little shops and buying a few souvenirs for her family, before going on to Cowes. There she mingled with the 'yachties' and, after buying an oil painting of a yacht by a local artist for her father, had a meal in a restaurant overlooking the busy Solent.

8

It was nearly nine o'clock when Kim returned, Joan had given her a key to the kitchen door, it was her intention to go straight to her room. As her car turned onto the drive she noticed Seb's Range Rover parked by the garage and the lounge lights were on. She would park around the back where Joan's husband parked his car, it was near the kitchen door and with a bit of luck she would be able to slip in unnoticed by the occupants in the lounge and go straight to bed.

Shutting the back door and locking it behind her as quietly as she could, Kim turned around and let out a scream, the key dropped from her hand, the sound of the metal hitting the cold stone tiles echoed in her ears as she stood staring at an irate Seb. He blocked the doorway, his arms folded across his large chest, his golden eyes wandering with contempt over her.
"Where the bloody hell have you been?"
"Why do you keep doing that to me!" she hollered back matching his anger.
"Doing what?" he asked narrowing his eyes.
"Creeping around and making me jump, anyway what's it to you where I've been?" she asked irately.
"Everything, it's polite to let others know where you are," he hissed walking into the room, closing the distance between them.
"I told Joan," she swallowed taking a step backwards in an effort to get away from his overpowering presence.
"Joan had gone by the time I returned, you should have left a note!"
"Seb what's going on, why are you shouting and who screamed?"
Seb and Kim turned around when the sound of the lilting Irish voice rang

around the room. Kim found herself looking into the most beautiful compassionate face she had ever seen. Although she didn't wear a veil, the dark blue outfit and large silver cross she wore told Kim she was a nun. So this was the love of Seb's life.
Seb ran a frustrated hand through his thick hair, and muttered an expletive. "Fiona, let me introduce you to Louise, Louise, Fiona."
There was no mistaking the look of mirth in the woman's big brown eyes as she summed up the situation. "Fiona, I'm pleased to meet you," Louise said ignoring Seb's obvious mood and pushing past him to shake hands with Kim. "Seb has told me a lot about you."
'I can imagine!' Kim smiled taking the offer of friendship, the way she felt about Seb, she shouldn't like this woman, but she did. "Pleased to meet you too Louise."
"Why don't the two of you go into the lounge, I'll make a coffee for us, have you eaten?" Louise asked Kim.
"Thank you yes, but..."
"No arguments, off you go and try to speak nicely to one another, sure it's no way to be carrying on!"
Seb and Kim were ushered out of the kitchen like small squabbling children.

Once in the lounge Seb turned, "How did you get hold of the car keys, did you manage to contact your friend?"
Kim watched the muscle in his cheek twitch and she realised he already knew the answer, "I received a parcel from Scotland this morning."
"He had your keys."
"Look Seb I don't wish to be rude to you, but I really don't see why I should allow you to cross-question me, what I do is no concern of yours! And I've got a bone to pick with you, you could have taken me to Yarmouth to catch a boat home on Monday, so why didn't you?" she asked in an effort to side-step the issue.
"Oh don't flatter yourself Fiona, the only reason I wanted you here was to prove to you that you are not in love with Alex!"
Clenching her fists into small tight balls she yelled back at him, "And how did you plan to prove that?"
Seb reddened a little and turned away. "My concern is for my brother, he doesn't deserve to be hurt again by your sort of woman!"
Kim grabbed his arm and forced him to turn back and face her. "Did it ever occur to you that by seducing his woman, you were the one causing him hurt? What would you know about 'my sort of woman', or any woman as far as that's concerned? You're different from other men."
His face went white, and he looked down at her restraining hand on his

arm with disdain. She had angered him to the limit, she knew and she didn't care, he asked for it.
"Different Fiona? In what way?" he asked softly.
"Cloistering yourself away from the real world pretending to be holier than thou...!"
"Lady, in comparison with you I'm a saint, a woman of your kind lets nothing get in her way, not even God's laws!"
"That's it, I've had enough!" Brushing past him towards the door she opened it, white faced she looked back at him.
"Do give my apologies to Louise, I have a headache and I'm going to bed!"
"You'll stay..."
"Seb! What's got into you, didn't you hear the poor wee thing say she has a headache?" Louise walked in with a tray of coffee cups and biscuits. "Perhaps I can get you some aspirins," she said with a concerned smile at Kim.
"Thank you Louise but I have some, I'm sorry I don't mean to be rude..."
"Not at all Fiona, off you go, I'll sort this bad tempered ol' bear out."

Kim heard Louise, this time her voice was raised, "I heard most of what you had to say to the poor girl, and you were tremendously rude what on earth has got into you..."
Kim didn't hang around to hear anymore and escaped to her room taking the stairs two at a time. She hadn't lied about the headache, her temples were throbbing. After taking two tablets and getting undressed, she crawled wearily into bed, tomorrow she would keep to her plan and spend the rest of the day touring, "and I don't care if it upsets him," she muttered thumping her pillow. Roll on Friday when Fiona and Alex would be here, and after seeing him eat humble pie she would be free to go!

Despite the heated argument with Seb, Kim managed to get a good night's sleep, she awoke to the sound of someone knocking on her door.
"Er...come in," she groaned sleepily as she sat up.
"Ah great you are awake. I've brought your breakfast, thought you'd like to have it in bed, how is the head, did you sleep alright?"
"The head is fine, and yes I slept like a log."
"Good, Seb has gone to see his solicitor, he thinks he'll be gone for most of the day so that leaves you and I, we'll have a girlie day, get to know one another." Louise chatted as she put a tray down on Kim's lap and walked over to the window to draw the curtains open. Kim ate her breakfast as she watched the lovely woman taking in the wonderful view.

"It's a lovely day the Lord has made, to be sure."
Kim grinned at her Irish lilt, "Looks it." 'Especially now you've told me Seb won't be here.' "Didn't you want to go with Seb?"
"Sure I did not! He's turned into a grumpy ol' bear, what would I be doing going around with him!" she stated indignantly walking back to the bed her arms folded across her ample breasts. "I only came here to be with Goldie."
Kim grinned some more as she munched on a slice of toast, she liked Louise, in fact she liked her a lot. "Yes thank you for loaning her, Tiny Tim is doing very well."
"Oh not at all, Goldie was pining for her lost puppy, Tiny Tim filled that space, he is a lovely wee dog."
Kim smiled, "I've got attached to him."
"So Seb told me! He pleaded with me to let him take Goldie, he didn't want to see you hurt."
"I don't think that was his reason," Kim uttered putting the woman right.
"You don't?"
"Never, Seb doesn't approve of me, doesn't even like me."
"What makes you think that?"
"You heard what he said last night."
"He didn't mean a word of it, he didn't know where you were and he was a little worried, besides he's got a lot on his plate at the moment!"
Kim stayed silent it wasn't worth quarrelling over, Seb hadn't been worried about her, he'd been worried that his plan to dishonour her in some way had been thwarted. Just then there was another knock on her door and Joan poked her head around the door. "Darren is downstairs in the kitchen, the badger is to be released this evening and he wondered if you would give its leg a final check sometime today?"
"Yes tell him to give me an hour to shower and dress."
Joan disappeared. "I'll leave you to get ready then," Louise said picking up the empty tray, "can I come and see the badger with you?"

Kim entered the kitchen, Louise was ready and waiting, together the two women walked over to the animal sanctuary.
"I understand the sanctuary was your idea," Kim said.
"Well sort of, I'm a teacher and I teach children with all sorts of difficulties in a convent school just outside of Portsmouth, many are autistic. If the children were good I used to allow them to see my animals at the convent, we have a few cats and two dogs. I began to notice that they opened up more, the animals were good therapy. So when Seb wrote to tell me he had returned to his father's place, I asked if he'd mind me bringing my class down one week-end to see the animals, his father kept

lots of farm animals after the collapse of the stud farm, it started from there. Seb noticed the change in the children too, and since then he's kept a small corner of the estate for this purpose. Only he extended it to bring local children, and children from the big cities. As well as doing something for children, his idea also helped injured wild animals, he is wonderful."
"He's very caring." Kim blinked as tears filled her eyes, 'but not to me' she thought sadly.
"He is the sweetest person I know!"
Kim fell silent, she couldn't agree.

Darren was mucking out the Pot Bellied Vietnamese pigs, and he put the broom down as soon as he saw the two women approaching.
"Hi," he called deftly leaping the small fence and ambling over to them, his blond hair bouncing around with each movement. "The wound on the fox is healing nicely, and Seb said if you agreed, it was fine to release the badger at dusk in the place where the police found him."
"If I agreed?" Kim questioned.
Darren nodded, "He respects your opinion!"
Kim raised her brows a fraction but refrained from commenting.

Kim nodded as she inspected the badger. "You're fine little man, we'll soon have you back with your family," she crooned over the creature, then turning to Darren. "I'd like to check on the fox while I'm here."
Darren led the two women to the cage and Kim looked at the fox's wound.
"That's good, do you think you can hold him or shall I sedate him while I remove the two big stitches, the rest are dissolvable?"
"He's only small, I'll give it a go," Darren said putting on a pair of large robust gloves.
"Well be careful, I wouldn't want you to be hurt!"
"No, its fine I have him."
Kim removed the stitches while Louise spoke soothingly to the creature and Darren held on to him tightly. "There you are little fellow," she spoke reassuringly to the animal as she took the last stitch out. "I think I'd like him to stay just one more night," she stated to Darren.
"Right you are, I'll put him back in his cage, it's a neat bit of sewing you did! Master Seb said he thought you knew more about animals than you were letting on!"
Kim bit her lip and turned away from the boy's deep blue eyes, she would have to be more careful.
"You were a veterinary nurse weren't you?" Louise asked.

"My father was a vet too, we learnt a lot from him, although his surgery was in the next village, people were always bringing injured animals to our home."
"So you followed in his footsteps?" Louise asked.
Kim rolled her sleeves up and washed her hands in the sink, "I did, thank you," she said taking the towel off Louise and changing the subject. "Would you like to go for a drive now, the weather looks good."
"I sure would, Seb said it was your first visit to the Island, what have you seen of it so far?"
Kim smiled, "Not a lot, the first day we...I went to Osborne House, yesterday I decided to see some of the Island."
"Oh and where did you go?" Louise asked linking her arm with Kim's as they strolled back towards the house.
"The Needles, Freshwater, Yarmouth and Cowes, but I spent longer in Yarmouth than I intended."
"You did?" Louise sounded surprised.
"I liked the little shops, and I sat and watched the boats, it was very relaxing."
Louise nodded, "Would you like to go to Godshill?"
"Godshill?"
"Yes it's a very pretty village in the centre of the Island, the church there is well worth a look round too.
"Sounds good to me," Kim agreed.
"That's settled then, its very high Church of England, you would be forgiven for thinking you'd entered a Catholic Church..."

9

"I'd forgotten how beautiful the Island was," Louise smiled as the car came to a halt on the driveway in front of Ashill Manor. "Thank you for taking me, I've really enjoyed myself."
"You're welcome, thank you for showing me around, I'm ready for my lunch, the walk along the river has given me an appetite!"
"Me too, race you to the kitchen."

The two girls burst noisily into the kitchen laughing, "I won," Kim screeched.
"Unfair, I think you have the advantage, you are younger and fitter," Louise puffed, as she bent over double to catch her breath.
"Oh come on, only by a couple of years, I..."
"What's going on?"
Turning round she came face to face with Seb, her laughter faded, "Seb, I thought..."
"Seb, you are home that's wonderful, your business didn't take you as long as you thought?"
"No," he shot Louise a gentle smile, Kim felt a pang of jealousy as she watched, astonished at the sudden transformation his face took on when he looked at the other woman. "It was quite straightforward, the man accepted my offer, I thought I'd have to barter. He's delivering the mare next week."
"Great," Louise chatted as she turned to put the kettle on.
"What have you two been doing?" he asked his eyes turning from Louise and coming to rest on Kim's face for a moment before they flickered insolently over her. He raised an eyebrow in askance as his eyes returned to her flushed face.
Kim felt as if he had actually touched her. "Will you excuse me?" Kim

asked trying to hide her breathlessness.
"Why?" he drawled lazily, enjoying her discomfort.
Looking down at her muddy trousers, "I need to change, I'm a little dirty!"
Seb raised his eyebrows again as he took in her muddy attire waiting for an explanation.
"We went to Godshill, then drove onto Newport Quay and went for a walk along the river Medina, Fiona slid down a track, got mud all over her derriere!" Louise explained with mirth in her eyes. "Ah, you should have seen the young men scrambling to her aid!"
"I can imagine," he muttered scathingly, loud enough for Kim's ears only. "Are you hurt?"
Kim groaned inwardly, 'why did Louise have to tell him!' Flicking her hair back off her flushed face she held his gaze. "Only my pride." With that she walked out of the kitchen.

Seb stood for a moment, staring at the closed door, 'has she any idea how beautiful she is?' he gulped. Suddenly aware that Louise was watching him he pulled himself together, "So you had a good time?" he enquired.
"Wonderful, she's lovely Seb!" Louise put a hand on his arm.
He pulled his arm away irritably, "You think so?"
"Yes, she seems a little familiar?"
"She bears a passing resemblance to one of the paintings in the Library."
"Which one?"
"Lady Rose's portrait! Did Joan tell you the old oak tree was struck by lightening, it was so badly damaged, John Downer had to fell it?"
Louise gave a shudder and frowned, "Spooky!"
"Coincidence, I don't believe in such nonsense!"
"Neither do I, I'll get us some lunch, Fiona and I are going to Carisbrooke Castle this afternoon, will you come with us?" she asked changing the subject.
"No," he snapped.
"That's not very nice, I go back to the convent on Saturday and I'd like to spend some time with you."
Seb sighed then smiled, "Alright, I'm sorry I'm being an old grump, it's just that the last few days have been a little hectic."

Kim scowled at him as they packed the lunch things away, she really didn't want to spend the rest of the day in his company. Louise had gone to change into something more appropriate for their trip out.
"We'll use my vehicle, I'll drive, I doubt whether your apology of a car

would be big enough for all of us!" Seb stated.
Stung into a retort, without thinking she blurted out, "I told you, it is not my car it's...a friends, and I can assure you that you would fit very well in my Range Rover back home!"
Seb narrowed his eyes, "You own a Range Rover?"
"Why shouldn't I?" she queried.
He shrugged, "No reason, it's just that Alex said you have only just taken up your engineering post!"
"So, engineering pays well these days!"
"So it does," he uttered his face breaking into a smile as Louise returned. "I was just saying, we would be better off in my car, Fiona's is too small for my bulk!"
"Good idea," Louise agreed. "Are we ready?"

After a light-hearted argument with Louise, Kim had stood, or rather sat her ground, and had managed to scamper into the back seat of the Range Rover. "I prefer to sit in the back!" she had assured the woman.

It took them less than half an hour to get to Carisbrooke village, stepping out of the vehicle she breathed in the crisp air and looked around. It was a pretty place overlooked by the imposing ancient structure of the Norman church. Although still early spring it was quite busy with tourists. Kim managed to lag a few steps behind Seb and Louise as they walked arm in arm towards the uneven steps that led up to the church and it's graveyard. 'She's welcome to him!' she huffed, lingering at the bottom of the steps and taking out the brochure that Fiona had picked up. She read over the historical narrative taking in the history of the place.
"Come on slow coach," Louise beckoned from the top, when she realised Kim wasn't with them.
Reluctantly Kim quickened her pace, "I'm coming."
She noticed Seb hadn't turned to see where she was and was just disappearing into the church!
To avoid being near him Kim turned and looked back at the view of the village from her elevated position. "It's a very peaceful place," she spoke softly to Louise.
"Hmm, though I think there have been times when it probably wasn't. Let's go inside and look around."

Kim chose to stroll around the opposite side to where Seb was and soon got engrossed with the plaques dedicated to different people down the ages, giving visitors a peek into bygone times. She shivered, like

most old churches it was extremely cold.
"Seen enough?" Louise asked.
"Yes, it's very cold in here!"
"Then lets join Seb in the sunshine, he's treating us to a tea and cream cake, then we're going to walk up to the castle. We are very fortunate, a jousting tournament is going on this week, we may well see some action!"

Seb took them to a small café in the village, where they had the choice of many different teas and cakes. Louise and Kim shared a pot of earl grey, and chose their cakes.
"Alex doesn't know you too well, does he?" Seb asked when she bit into a calorie laden bun.
"H-how do you mean?" she asked, licking the icing sugar from her lips.
He watched the action through narrowed eyes, "He told me you counted your calories remember? I've seen no evidence of this."
"I'm on holiday, I'm allowed!"
"Ah, I stand corrected," he said putting his knife down on the plate and wiping his mouth on a napkin.
"Everyone indulges on holiday," Louise chipped in seemingly unaware of the crackling tension between her two friends. "Did you see that medieval…"

Kim cut herself off from their conversation, concentrating on eating the bun with as much finesse as she could muster, it was extremely sticky and creamy.
"That was wonderful, I'm just going to the Ladies," Louise stated.
Before Kim could offer to go with her, Louise was off, leaving Kim alone with Seb.
She finished her bun, "Thank you, it was delicious," she said.
Seb leaned across to her and picked up her napkin. Her large blue eyes widened as his long fingers cupped her chin and lifted it up, while his other hand wiped her chin. "You have cream on your face!" he smiled, as he stared into her eyes his face came nearer to hers as if some unknown force were drawing them together, a force neither seemed able to resist.
"Right are we ready…" Louise's question hung in mid air.
Abruptly Seb let go of her chin, threw the napkin down on the plate, and scraping his chair back, stood up, "I'll see to the bill," he muttered.
Red faced Kim got up and walked out of the tearoom, head held high. 'He was going to kiss me!' she thought touching her lips, which felt like he already had.
Kim was grateful to Louise, who chatted excitedly as they explored

the medieval castle with its impressive battlements. If she thought the views were breathtaking along the Military Road into Freshwater, this topped it! It was such a clear day, you could see for miles. Even Southampton and Portsmouth were clearly visible.
"The position was excellent, they could see immediately if anyone was invading from the mainland!" Seb muttered coming to stand by her side.
"It's very...what's the word?"
"Indescribable!" he proffered mockingly.
She giggled and smiled up into his face, "That's the word!"
Their eyes met and he sucked in his breath, for a moment totally lost for words himself.
"The tournament is starting in about half an hour, shall we go down to the field?" Louise interrupted breaking the spell that had been cast over them.
"Good idea," Seb murmured as he led the way down the worn stone steps, "Mind how you go, they are a little precarious!" he warned both of them.

The field where the pageant was being held was filling up fast, "Find yourselves a good seat," Seb told them. "I'm just going to have a word with an old friend I've just seen, he helps run the jousting tournament."
"No Seb you dare!" Louise challenged.
He turned around and continued to walk backwards away from them, his normally dour face broke into a broad grin, and Kim watched amazed at the transformation. "Don't dare me Louise." With that he was gone.
"What was that about?" Kim asked her friend.
"Hopefully nothing, let's get one of those front seats near the tents," Louise muttered as she edged her way forward in the crowd.

The jousting tournament was just beginning as they sat down on the wooden benches. Louise chose a good seat near the changing tents where the combatants were coming out dressed as medieval knights and mounting their big strong horses.
"Oh no! I knew he would do that!" Louise groaned as she watched a knight dressed in white come out of the tent. "Seb!" she shouted.
The knight turned, "Its Seb!" Kim stated unnecessarily.
With a nonchalant air he ambled over to them, unhindered by the weight of the armour, the visor on his helmet was closed, Kim sucked in her breath as he stared out from the square holes of the armour, his golden eyes were burning into hers. He lifted an ironclad hand towards her and with one yank, grabbed the silk scarf she wore loosely around her neck.
"A woman usually gave the knight she wanted to win her colours, I'll take this, unless you want me to lose?" he voice resonated around the metal

helmet.
"O-of course I-I want you to win," she mumbled overcome by a sudden shyness. 'He must have known that the 'woman' who gave her knight her colour, was his lover also!' she thought coyly.
Louise giggled. "Seb, stop teasing Fiona!"
"Why should I? She likes to tease me!" he stated seductively, tucking the scarf into his belt. "Wish me luck!" he asked bowing low to them and walking away.

Kim watched as he mounted a big white horse helped by other strong men, a lance was put into his hand. He immediately took her scarf off his belt and tied it round the end of the lance. As if he sensed she was looking his head turned to her, and her heart flipped. She knew then that he was her knight, her knight in shining white armour.
"Doesn't he look the part?" Louise asked grasping her arm.
Kim nodded, she felt strange, his look had burnt into her, and the atmosphere of the place did strange things to her emotions, causing a feeling of déjà vu. She didn't believe in reincarnation but for a split second she had imaged that she had known him from another life, that she had seen him in armour before! Shaking herself she pretended to look at the different shields adorning the trees around them.

Unable to watch, Kim covered her eyes, as the horse's hooves thundered over the ground either side of a stout rope, the noise resounding through the ground they were sitting on, galloping at breakneck speed towards the opponent.
"They've missed one another!" Louise told her obligingly.
Kim took a peek between her fingers and swallowed as they turned to go into combat again, then covered her eyes when the horses charged at one another.
An unexplainable foreboding settled over her, she would lose him and never see him again! Kim could stand it no more, in fear for his safety she stood up and walked away, trying to stem the sudden rush of tears, Louise ran after her with concern in her face. "Seb's won, his opponent is off his horse!" Louise shouted to make herself heard above the roar of the crowd.
"Is he hurt?" she asked brushing a tear away with an unsteady hand.
"No, Seb's just helped him up and they are walking off together."
Kim wasn't thinking of the other man! "Thank goodness for that!" She let out a faltering breath as she joined in the applause. "I didn't know Seb was any good at jousting!"
"You shouldn't get so upset, he's an ace," Louise stated putting a friendly

arm around her, bringing her back to the seat and, giving her a handkerchief, made her sit down. "He's been involved with the group who put on the shows for years, his father used to look after their horses in his stables. At first Seb was happy just to watch them practice, but as he got older he begged them to let him get involved. He always was a daredevil!"
"I'm sorry, it's just that...it's a little frightening...and I was concerned that someone would get hurt."
"That someone being Seb?"
"No," she denied indignantly, "I was worried for the horses!"
Grateful it was over, Kim blew her nose and wiped her face. "Do I look alright?" she asked her friend.
"Fine," Louise assured her. "They are holding an exhibition of medieval armour over there," Louise declared pointing to a tent. "Let's go and have a closer look while we wait for Seb."

They walked over to a tent that housed a tremendous array of arms and armour.
Louise was a mine of information, and after an enjoyable wander around the magnificent display of medieval art, Seb joined them.
"Your colours bought me success!" he stated bowing low as he handed her scarf back.
"Thank you."
"Did you enjoy seeing me win?"
"I covered my eyes," she answered wryly.
"She couldn't bear to see you hurt, you caused her some anxiety!" Louise chipped in.
"Really?" Seb asked raising his brows.
"I was worried about the horses," she stated changing the subject. "Have you seen this tapestry Louise?"
As Kim turned towards her friend, Seb caught her arm and turned her around, one long finger lifted her chin making her look him in the eye. "You look as if you've been crying!"
"Don't be so ridiculous, I...the grass...I suffer from hay fever!"
Contesting her excuse, "This time of year? Were you shedding tears for me? Could it be that you were concerned for my safety and not the horses?"
"Seb stop teasing the girl, she's been sneezing away, sure she has, they've been cutting the grass!" Louise came to her rescue.
"Hmm," Seb said unconvinced. Luckily his mobile phone beeped and, letting her go, he walked away from the hubbub of noise to answer it, but not before she'd seen the laughter in his eyes. It took her all her time not

to physically attack the man.
"Come on, you must see the donkeys at the well," Louise insisted seeing the fury in her face.

Seb was waiting by the exit for them and smiled at Louise as she linked her arm in his. "Have you seen all you wanted to?" he asked.
"I have, have you Fiona?"
"Yes, thank you," she whispered and looked away as his smile disappeared into a dark brooding frown when his eyes fell of her.
"The call was from Alex," he was speaking to Louise, but Kim knew he was saying it for her benefit.
"Is he alright?" Louise asked.
"Fine, he's won the business deal for me."
"Good," she beamed, "Did you hear that Fiona?"
"Aren't you going to ask me if he's alright, he's your lover after all?" Seb turned to Kim.
"No need I heard you tell Louise that he was fine!"
"For a lover, you are very cool towards him!" he stated softly so that only Kim heard.
She coloured and refused to rise to the bait, "Perhaps in company, but when we're alone, well...you would never describe us as...cool!"
His glare cut through her as he turned and strode angrily on ahead. Louise kept up with him, but Kim held back, walking a few paces behind, not wishing to see his look of condemnation or hear his conversation.
"I'll sit in the back this time," Louise shouted back to her and got in before Kim could argue.
Seb held the door open for her, "I don't bite, get in!" he ordered uttering an oath under his breath when he saw her scowl.

Kim sat gloomily staring out of the window, you could have cut the atmosphere in the car with a knife, luckily, Louise seemed totally unaware of it and kept up a light-hearted banter for the duration of the journey home.

"Dinner will be a little formal, I have a few guests coming," Seb uttered curtly as he held both car doors open for Louise and Kim.
"I'll put on my best habit!" Louise giggled as she looped her arm in Kim's and walked to the front door.
"How formal is 'a little formal'?" Kim asked looking a little worried, "I didn't bring any evening wear with me!"
Seb had overheard their discussion, "Don't worry, my mother liked to play the Lady of the Manor, she entertained a lot and kept an array of

evening gowns for unprepared guests, Louise will show you where they are while I check the puppies."

"I can't wear this it's outrageous!" Kim stated.
"Why on earth not, you look really beautiful, the blue catches the colour of your eyes."
"Don't you think I ought to wear something a little bit more..." she asked pulling the low top of the figure hugging velvet sheath up a little.
"I do not! I may be a nun but I'm a great believer in using what the Almighty gave you, remember the parable of the talents!"
Unconvinced, Kim worried the soft flesh of her mouth as she gazed back at her reflection. She had never worn such an elegant gown. It was a rich sapphire blue, sleeveless and cut on the bias so that it fell elegantly over her curvy figure. "I'll be cold in this," she said rubbing her bare arms.
"No you won't, it comes with this little bolero top."
Louise held the cropped long sleeved top up for her to slip on, "There, now don't you look a picture?"
"I don't recognise myself," she whispered as she gaped at the seductive creature looking back at her in the long mirror. Louise had styled her hair into curling waves on top of her head, revealing her long swan like neck.

Much to Kim's surprise Louise selected a gown for herself, it was a short sleeved empire line, in rich red velvet.
"What do you think?"
"Great you look lovely Louise, but I thought..."
"Thought that we aren't allowed to look great?"
"Well yes..."
"My order is very modern it was founded in America, we are allowed to choose our own clothes. Our mother superior abhors the stupid impractical gowns that most nuns' wear," she grimaced. "We see a need to mingle with the rich just as much as the poor, in fact they are sometimes in more need of hearing the good news! And to be with them we have to dress accordingly! As long as we don't look too..."
"See, how can I wear this!"
"Fiona, you forget, you're in the market for marriage, I am married to God, besides I haven't got your wonderful figure, now not another word!

10

Nervously she hung back behind Louise as her huge eyes adjusted to the dim light of the elegant reception area that led to the dining room. It was lit by thousands of candles. If this was Seb's idea of a few guests, well, the room was crowded!

"Come on, don't be shy, I'll introduce you to Seb's Aunt and Uncle, you'll love them," Louise whispered as she dragged the coy Kim towards an elderly couple. "Aunt Georgia, Uncle Ted, I'd like to introduce you to Fiona, she's staying here for a few days, with Seb.

No sooner had she been introduced, Louise was whisked away by someone, while Kim was left to shake hands with Seb's relatives, "How do you do."

"Very well, and you my dear, have you known Seb long?"

"I..."

"Long enough Auntie, so stop digging."

Kim trembled as she felt Seb's strong cool hands cover her shoulders, giving her a warning squeeze he whispered in her ear loud enough for the older woman to overhear. "Say nothing, Auntie likes to pry into my private life!"

"Seb is very unkind to me! I only have his good interest at heart," Aunt Georgia protested, unabashed by his rudeness.

Seb chuckled back at the woman. "I'm sure you have, and I appreciate your care Auntie, but my life is my own!" he stated pulling Kim back into his muscled body. She didn't resist, somehow she felt safe as his deep voice thundered over her head and his breath stirred the stray tendrils of her hair.

"So now you've already met my friend, the delectable Fiona, may I take her away to introduce her to my other guests?"

Uncle Ted bowed low as he excused them.

"For the moment, but I expect you to bring her back," Aunt Georgia stated grinning good-naturedly back at her nephew, "I'm intrigued!"
Kim sucked in her breath as he came and stood by her side, his hand dropping intimately to her waist. The vision before her made her heart pound in her chest as she stared up at him, he was dressed in a black dinner jacket and looked darkly handsome, his tawny eyes shimmered like molten gold in the candle light. It amazed her that she hadn't spotted him when they first entered the room he was head and shoulders taller than any other man.
A lazy sexy smile tugged at his lips and his eyes never left Kim's face, "Of course, Aunt Georgia, when I've warned her about the way you gossip!" he smiled taking his Aunt's hand and raising it to his lips, before he led Kim away.

"You were very rude to your Aunt," Kim rebuked him.
Seb's grin broke out into a low soft chuckle, "Auntie and I always spar around with words, I love her to bits and she knows it. Now the chief inspector of the Island police is here tonight, Trisha has changed her statement and has told the police that she thinks her husband knew who the intruder was. Her solicitor is taking her allegations very seriously, so I'm introducing you as my friend, don't you dare mention Alex, do you hear." he warned when they were out of earshot.
"I hear," she whispered fearing for Alex and her sister.

Kim fixed a sociable smile to her lips as Seb snaked his arm around her waist and whisked her around the room, introducing her to a sea of faces, before introducing her to the chief inspector, David Hardy. Her heart was thundering in her breast as she tried to concentrate on the introduction and not on the man beside her, nor his hand that was gently caressing the curve of her waist.
David chatted politely to her while Seb spoke to the man's wife, although Kim was very aware that Seb's concentration was trained on the conversation she was having with the man.
"I understand you are a family friend?"
"Yes," Kim agreed trying not to look Seb in the eye.
"You were staying at the cottage before the storm brought down the telephone lines?"
"I-I was, then Seb's dog developed a problem and couldn't feed her puppy's so I offered to help."
"Ah, that would explain why Seb didn't just loan you his mobile phone until the engineers could fix the phone!"
Kim frowned, 'Mobile phone? Of course, it hadn't registered when Seb

had used it earlier on today. What was going on? The man had a mobile phone!'
"Doesn't work in that area, and because my line had been down, the battery had run flat," Seb cut in with a smile before he let go of her waist and acknowledged another guest.
"I understand there were two young women staying at the cottage, did your friend go home?" David enquired.
Kim nearly choked on her drink, she glanced up at Seb, who luckily for her was deep in conversation with David's wife and the other guest, and hadn't heard. She turned away from Seb and muttered, "My sister, she only came for the week-end, she's gone on to stay further north with a friend," she said as quietly as she could, before changing the subject. She sighed with relief when Seb took her back to Louise, leaving them so he could greet some late arrivals.

They didn't see Seb until the dinner gong sounded and he walked over to them, bowing low he invited them both to link their arms in his, "Allow me to escort you to your seats. In jousting the winning knight gets to dance with the woman who spurred him on to win, but seeing that there is no dance."
He shrugged his broad shoulders apologetically, "I will take you both to dinner," he drawled, holding out an arm to each of them, a cautioning look in his eyes told Kim she was not to disobey. With no choice but to put her arm through his, Louise giggled and linked her arm in his free one, "Now you are like a pot with two handles!"
"Indeed I am," he replied taking them through.

Kim looked in awe at the elegant table before her, set for at least sixty guests. Taking her hand away from his arm she turned to go down the table. To her consternation he held her back, "Oh no sweetheart, you are near the top, next to me, remember I won the joust, it is my reward!" Reluctantly Kim took her seat next to Seb at the head, and an elderly gentleman, whose name escaped her, sat to her right. Louise was on Seb's left, with Uncle Ted next to her.

Kim sat tensely as the waitresses served the first course, a mixture of chicken and exotic fruits, sprinkled with a Jamaican herbs, it was delicious but Kim couldn't relax enough to enjoy it. The chief inspector and his wife were sat on the other side of the man next to her, she was terrified that he would say something more about her sister, and the nearness of Seb didn't help either.
Even though the salmon en-croute was mouth-wateringly tasty, to Kim it

could have been made of cardboard. She pushed it around the plate in the hope it would decrease in size.
"Not to your taste, or are you trying to save the calories?" Seb whispered his piercing eyes delving deeply into hers.
"I'm sorry, its delicious but maybe I shouldn't have eaten such a big cream bun!" she excused herself, looking away from the handsome face.
"Hmm," he conceded, "Have you spoken to Peter yet?"
"Peter?"
"The gentleman to your right."
"No, I couldn't remember his name," she whispered back.
"Ah, he arrived late, I didn't introduce you I'm sorry! Let me make amends, Peter?"
The gentleman turned to speak to Seb. "Peter this is the young lady I told you about, the one that helped me with the puppies and saw to the fox the police bought in the other day!" He turned to Kim, "Peter is the local vet," he offered.
Peter smiled at her. "You did a marvellous job on the fox, I understand you are going with Darren tomorrow evening to release it back into the wild?"
"Yes, he wasn't that badly injured."
"Even so, for a veterinary nurse you did exceedingly well, I wouldn't expect one of my nurses to be able to cope with what you did!" the man said with a bumptious air, casting a knowing look at Seb.
Kim was aware that Seb was watching her reaction and listening to every word with more than just a fleeting interest, it was as if he were trying to catch her out. What medical treatment she did administer was no more than a good nurse was capable of, Fiona would and could have dealt with the fox.
Aware that all eyes were on her, it was with a gleam in her eye that she answered. "Ah but I have the advantage, Peter," Kim took delight in telling the rather pompous old man, "My father is a vet, I was brought up with a knowledge of how to minister to injured animals!"
"We have animal nurses at the convent Peter, no offence to Fiona, but they are just as competent, your nurses were trained thirty years ago, when men didn't allow women to learn too much, goodness they might have taken over!" Louise uttered tartly, coming to her rescue. Kim heard Seb suck in his breath at the other woman's insult, one thing was blatantly obvious, he hadn't bargained on Louise taking her side.
"True," Peter acknowledged casting another look at Seb before he turned away wearied with the whole episode.
"Now stop teasing Fiona," Louise admonished casting Seb a caustic look.
"Ah but I enjoy teasing Fiona," he murmured in a soft sexy laugh as he

reached up and touched Kim's hot cheek.
She jerked away from his caress, "If that is all you have to please you then Sir, you lead a very boring life!" Kim hissed back at him.
He lent towards her, "Maybe you could liven it up?" he suggested softly.
Kim glanced around the table, had others heard what he said? Everyone was engrossed with his or her own conversation; even Louise was deep in discussion with his Uncle.
"I'm sorry Louise is right I shouldn't tease, truce?" he begged, seeing her confusion. "Come, enjoy the food, I promise I won't torment you anymore, besides you've got to have an appetite for the next course, its raspberry Pavlova, and Alex told me it is your favourite."
Kim swallowed down a groan it might be Fiona's favourite but she hated raspberries. 'Too bad,' an inner voice reminded her, 'you'll have to enjoy them tonight!'

The evening was the longest Kim had ever experienced, after dinner they had all retired to the reception area, and Aunt Georgia had collared her. She found herself bombarded with impertinent questions about her and Seb, until Seb, seeing her predicament, came to her rescue and whisked her away to speak to another guest, Seb's lawyer and his wife. By the end of the evening Kim's brain was whirring as she tried to avoid all the questions thrown at her by nearly everyone. It seemed Seb had exaggerated when he'd said he often had 'guests' staying, well not exaggerated, more distorted when he failed to tell her they were usually all married couples! A single available woman apparently was virtually unheard of, hence his guests inquisitiveness!

Towards the end of the evening, wearied and drained, Kim saw her chance to slip out without causing offence. Louise had disappeared and Seb was seeing some of his guests off. After spending some time with the puppies, Kim made her way to the hall, the reception area was now deserted. The last of the guests were gone, she heard car doors slamming as cheerful voices the other side of the front door said their goodnights and drove off into the night.
Hearing the sound of a mobile phone ringing then Seb's dark velvety voice getting nearer, Kim ran quickly up the stairs, she was halfway up when he broke the silence, "Wait, Fiona!"

Kim turned round to see Seb walking through the double front doors holding his mobile phone to his ear, his face was a stern mask.
'Bad timing,' she told herself stopping at his demand.
"I have Alex on the phone, he wants to talk to you, here take it!" he

commanded holding the phone towards her.
Kim had no alternative but to come down, his stormy eyes watching her every step. With heart thumping loudly she descended slowly, determined that he wasn't going to detect her chagrin.

She would have made it, but for the heel of her high stiletto. With a cry of consternation she fell forward as it caught in the hem of her gown. An expletive escaped from his mouth as he caught her and pulled her fiercely against his hard body. For a moment all was still then, with a groan, his hand descended down her spine to her buttocks, his fingers spread out to hold her masterly against him. Somewhere in the distance she heard a bleep as he clicked the phone off. Her arms wound around his neck and she moaned as his mouth brushed savagely against hers. His kiss was cruel, demanding, but she offered no resistance. She knew he was inflicting some sort of chastisement on her, his words confirmed it as he moved his mouth away from hers and whispered huskily. "Quite the little actress are you not? If you wanted me that much you didn't have to risk an injury by falling into my arms, you know I want you, and don't worry about Alex hearing what a little tart you really are, I turned the phone off."
Spontaneously her hand went up and slapped his arrogant face, there was silence as they stared at one another, Kim felt the tears prickling in her eyes as she watched a red mark appear on his cheek in the shape of her hand, but he showed no emotion.
"I suppose you think I deserved that?" he uttered tonelessly.
Resting her hands on his shoulders she lowered her head and shut her eyes.
"Nothing to say?"
"You deserved it," she whispered.
"You don't think that you are behaving badly?"
"No y-you k-kissed me!"
She felt the low rumble of laughter as he held her tightly against his broad chest, "Oh don't deceive yourself sweetheart, I am aware of the game you are playing, conquering the unconquerable. In fact I think you would gloat if I told you that you tempt me beyond endurance!" he said in a hoarse voice
"Sir you tempt yourself, I hate..."
The shrill tones of the telephone ringing silenced her. "Saved by the bell?" he laughed softly handing her the mobile. "Better go into the lounge and answer it, it will be your lover, I would hate to overhear your lies to him!"

11

"Good morning," Kim mumbled as she walked into the kitchen the following morning.
"Good morning," Louise and Joan answered in unison, if they noticed the dark rings under her eyes and her pale face, they never mentioned it.
"No Seb?" Kim inquired tentatively.
"No, he left ages ago, he'll be gone for most of the day, good job too, he was in an awful grump!" Louise answered nonchalantly.
Kim sighed with relief as she sat down at the table, after last night she didn't think she could face him again, well not until he knew the truth.
"I was planning to do some more touring today, would you like to come with me?" she asked Louise.
"I'd love to, in fact I was going to suggest it, make the most of my freedom. Listen Fiona," she said sitting down next to her and lowering her voice when Joan disappeared into the garden. "I need to speak to you about something."
"Sounds intriguing," Kim queried, taking a bite from her toast, "that something being Seb I take it?"
"It is, I'll get a picnic lunch together while you finish your breakfast and get yourself ready."

An hour later they were on the road, Louise sat next to her acting as navigator. Louise had chosen the venue, a local beauty spot, which overlooked the Solent.
"We can have our lunch in the picnic area if this weather continues," Louise chatted happily. "We can talk there without being interrupted."
Kim nodded a little amazed that this woman wanted to talk to her about Seb, what on earth could she possibly have to say to her. Unless Seb had asked her to tell her to leave Alex alone, maybe he had told her about

what happened between them last night!

"That's the place," Louise stated pointing to an old ruin.
Indicating, Kim turned the vehicle into the deserted picnic area. The sun was extremely warm, so they decided to have their sandwiches 'El Fresco'.
They chatted about this and that until they had finished their lunch, Louise poured out two coffees from a flask. "Sugar?" she asked.
Kim shook her head and thanked her as Louise handed her the cup.
"Right I expect you're wondering why I want to talk to you?" she said straddling the wooden bench so she could face Kim.
Kim looked straight ahead, keeping her face and emotions concealed. "I must say I'm intrigued but if you are going to lecture me and ask me to stop seeing Alex..."
Louise put her hand on Kim's arm and stated indignantly, "I am not! I want to tell you about Seb and me."
Kim looked down at the steaming cup of coffee before her, attempting to hide the pain that she knew was in her eyes. "You and Seb are still an item then?"
The soft bubble of laughter that floated in the air made Kim look up in surprise into Louise's bright eyes.
"No!" she cried incredulously. "We *were* an item a long time ago, we were just kids. You see, Fiona, I knew I was called, I wanted to be a nun ever since I could remember. Seb and I have known one another since we were children, my parents took their holidays here, we used to stay at Rose cottage, Seb's father rented it out in the summer. Our respective parents became great friends. My father was a Doctor, and Alex had a bad accident when he was five."
"What happened?"
" Seb and Alex disobeyed their father and went into the stables, they were playing hide and seek. Alex hid in a pen, which housed an aggressive stallion, it was a wonder he wasn't killed! My father was taking a walk when he heard Seb screaming for help."
"How awful."
"It was for Seb, his mother blamed him, he was the eldest and should have known better, he was only seven!" she stated dryly.
Kim swallowed, it made more sense of Seb's anger when he'd found her in Black Fury's pen the other night!"
Louise went on, "After that event my parents were invited to stay at Ashill Manor, and my brother and I spent nearly all our school holidays here. When Seb and Alex got older, they used to come to us for holidays in Ireland. We became attracted to each other in our teens, unfortunately

I got more deeply involved with him than I intended, mine was puppy love. I'm afraid Seb fell heavier than I did. The poor man was heartbroken when I told him I was going into a convent."

She took a sip of coffee before she continued, Kim noticed her eyes became distant. "I love him Fiona, but only as a brother that's all, I never meant to hurt him, but regrettably I did. The same year I entered the convent they found out I had cancer of the womb, I had a successful hysterectomy and thanks be to God, I've had no reoccurrence, that was over twelve years ago. To cut a long story short, Seb found out and thought I'd become a nun because I couldn't have his children, no matter how hard I tried to convince him this was not the case. I think that idea made it easier to accept that I turned him down, his pride took an awful knocking. Eventually I took my final vows and in a fit of pique he entered Quarr Abbey vowing that if I wouldn't marry him then he too would never marry. He was young, we were both only twenty. I'd prayed he would change his mind, I knew, he had no calling to the priesthood, God made him to be a husband and father. It seems God took over and answered my prayers, his father needed his help, Alex didn't get on with the old fellow they were too alike. Oh not in looks but in personality."

"So Seb came home," Kim said.

Louise inclined her head slightly as she looked ahead. "There was no one else. When Seb's religious elders heard he was needed, they insisted that the godly thing to do was for Seb to go home and help his father, they suggested he put his priestly vocation on hold. I think deep down they knew he wasn't cut out for it. He left the Abbey just before he was due to take his final vows, thank God!"

"So he...he isn't a monk?" Kim whispered the feeling of relief soon overcome by anger at his pretence.

"No, well not yet, he could have gone back last year, now he's free of his family duty...but he didn't."

"He said he's training Alex up to take over Ashill Manor so he can continue with his vocation!" Kim said flatly.

"He told you that?"

"Yes."

A knowing smile tugged at Louise's mouth, "You confuse him, I noticed the way he looks at you. I have never seen him so angry," she smiled. "Boy, when you came home late the first night I was there! He went crazy, Darren told him he'd seen you drive off in your car. He paced the floor all the evening."

"Why?"

"Fiona don't you see? He thought you'd left!"

"Oh, I see, it was only because Seb promised Alex he'd keep me here

until he returned from Scotland."
"Phooey!" she spat out, "it's got nothing to do with Alex!"
"What are you saying?" Kim asked feeling her face getting redder.
"The air practically crackled around the pair of you last night, he couldn't take his eyes off you when you walked into the reception room and I've a confession to make."
"Oh!"
"I deliberately encouraged you to wear the blue dress last night, knowing the neck line and the colour was identical to the dress Lady Rose was wearing in her portrait."
"I don't know what you're talking about!"
"Lady Rose, her ghost haunts Rose Cottage!"
"I still don't understand..."
"He hasn't shown you the portrait of her?"
"I didn't know there was a portrait."
"The legend says..."
"Yes the tree surgeon told me the story..."
"You bear a remarkable likeness to Lady Rose!"
"I do? How strange, I'd like to see the painting."
"I'll show you when we get back." Louise put her head to one side and leaned forward so she could look into Kim's eyes, "You are in love with him aren't you Fiona?"
"No...I...Yes," she admitted lowering her head in shame and confusion. "And you wouldn't believe the mess I'm in."
"Try me," the saintly woman invited.

"So let me get this straight, your real name is Kim, you *are* a fully qualified vet, and Fiona is your twin sister. She is with Alex in Scotland at this very moment?" Louise asked watching the other woman pacing up and down before her.
"Yes, somehow I've found myself in this stupid predicament, I should never have agreed, I didn't agree! Honestly Louise, I was forced into it. Now Seb thinks I'm committing adultery with his brother, and making passes at him too."
"Making passes?"
"I-I we've kissed a few times, I think on every occasion I led him on!" Kim gulped and sat down heavily on the wooden bench hanging her head in shame.
"Did you now and who said you led him on?"
"He did."
Louise raised her eyebrows in disbelief and controlling the smile on her face with great difficulty, put an arm around the tortured girl's shoulders.

"Cheer up, Alex and Fiona will be home tonight and the truth will be told by all."
"Then the fireworks will start, Seb will be livid!" Kim groaned.
"He'll be livid with Alex," she agreed.
"And me!" Kim added.
"I don't see why, you are just as much a victim as he is. I'll pray for all of you, you'll see, it will all be alright!"
"I admire you confidence!"
"Kim, I want you to promise me something."
"Depends what it is first, I'm in enough trouble for promising things to people!"
"I can't guarantee it won't be easy, and God forgive me if I'm wrong, but I know Seb is strongly attracted to you, if not already in love with you! I want you to promise that you'll try your best to win his love..."
"What are you saying..."
"I'm asking you to make him see that he's a man cut out for marriage, I want you to make him change his mind, and forget his vow!"
Kim looked horrified, "I can't, suppose you are wrong? You shouldn't have asked me that!"
"I don't think I've misjudged the situation, but if you think I have, forget I ever mentioned it, I only asked you because I didn't want Seb to make the biggest mistake of his life! Come on, let's enjoy the rest of the day."

It was late afternoon when they eventually arrived home, Kim walked in the kitchen to make a drink while Louise went into Seb's study to make a call to her convent, to tell them what time she was arriving back.
Kim sucked in her breath, Seb was sat at the table drinking coffee and reading a newspaper, he looked up and scowled, shook the paper aggressively and held it high. She heard his snort, 'I don't want to see your face either,' she huffed as she moved over to the kettle busying herself making coffee for herself and Louise, stung by his rudeness. The atmosphere was electric, and she fought the urge to rip the paper out of his hands. The kettle came to the boil and she turned away from him to pour the water in the mugs. "Rude pig!" she muttered, thinking he wouldn't hear.
"Did you speak?" he asked making her jump.
"Not to you!" she answered childishly.
Her heart thumped when she heard his fist hit the oak table as he tossed the paper down and scraped the chair back. "I heard what you called me, and ill-manners don't become you Fiona." He was moving over to her, 'why didn't you keep your mouth shut?' she scolded herself rooted to the

spot with fear, feeling her face fuse with colour.

"Hi Seb, had a good day?" Louise breezed in.
Seb stopped in his tracks scowled and stuffed his hands into his trouser pockets, Kim breathed out in relief, the last thing she needed was another confrontation with him.
"Hi Louise, yes it was great, one of the projects has just been approved of by the local council, Brother Joseph was pleased." In a second his mood swung from ferocious to light and amiable as he chatted to Louise, effectively pushing Kim out of the conversation.
Muttering her excuses, which to her knowledge neither had heard, she picked up her coffee and walked quickly up to her room.

Shutting the bedroom door she leant against it, glad of the silence, she needed to be alone with the information Louise had given her about Seb not being a monk. Thinking back he had never said he was, all he'd said was that he'd been in a monastery. No, that was not strictly true, when they'd kissed the second time he had definitely said that he'd taken a vow! Realisation suddenly hit her, the vow he and Louise were talking about was the vow he'd made to her, not the priestly vows! But on the other hand, she thought rubbing her aching temples, he had said that he had plans to hand over the estate to Alex so that he could pursue his own vocation!
Taking in a deep breath she flopped down on the bed and shut her eyes, "I don't know!" she exclaimed to herself, life was getting so difficult. Where would she go from here? 'Take one step at a time,' she recalled her father's sound advice, oh how she longed to speak to him, he was so wise, and he would know what to do. 'Maybe you'll get your wish sooner than you think,' she grimaced at the thought, Alex and Fiona would be home around ten o'clock tonight, then she would know her fate. Seb would probably send them all packing for their deceit. The thought of his anger and disappointment in her caused a tear to trickle down her cheek.

Opening her eyes she held up her arm to look at her wristwatch, "Oh goodness," she exclaimed getting off the bed. It was six o'clock and she was supposed to be accompanying Darren at half past to release the fox. Quickly changing into jeans and a jumper she redid her makeup, and brushed her hair until it shone. Picking up her sheepskin jacket she left the room.

"Hi I was just coming up to tell you its time to return the fox to the wilds," Louise stated as Kim walked into the kitchen.

"Sorry I fell asleep, all this country air," she said flippantly.
"Probably needed it, both you and Seb look like you haven't slept for a week!" she tutted. "Thank goodness you only had to feed the puppies for two days."
"Indeed," Seb drawled as he came into the kitchen from the back door, "Did you want to check the fox over before we release him?" he turned towards Kim but avoided eye contact.
'Why did he have to come!' she moaned to herself. "Yes," she snapped brushing past him into the yard, and walking swiftly over to the farm surgery.

"You'll do!" she whispered to the creature as she gave him a thorough check over and gave him the last dose of antibiotics while Darren held him. Seb hovered over her his arms folded over his large chest, watching her every move with suspicion in his eyes. 'Well only another four hours and you'll know the truth!' she reminded herself, casting him a dark frown.
"Ready?" he asked.
Kim nodded and stood back while Seb helped Darren to put the animal into a wire basket. Kim walked away and headed for the Range Rover with Louise and climbed into the back seat, she had no intention of sitting anywhere near him!

Her anger with Seb was pushed to the back of her mind as they took the animal to the spot where he was found, she held her breath as Seb and Darren opened the basket. The creature crept tentatively out of the cage, sniffing his way around until he'd picked up his scent, without a backward glance he was off into the night.
"He's free!" Kim whispered close to tears, the big man standing by the side of her looked down at her, a strange look in his eyes.
"It's a good feeling, isn't it?" Seb muttered huskily.
Forgetting to be cross with him, her watery eyes shone up into his, "Yes...It's wonderful, so worthwhile!"
He held her gaze for a long while, his golden eyes piercing into her very soul. Kim swallowed and dropped her gaze as an emotion swamped her making her feel very out of her depth.
"Let's go!" Seb spoke sharply, picking up the empty basket and turning away.

Kim's heart skipped a beat when she saw a big shiny black BMW on the drive as Seb drove the Range Rover through the big double gates, Alex and Fiona were back, they were early! By the time Seb had pulled

on the handbrake Kim was trembling with nerves. The enormity of what she had done weighed heavily on her shoulders, Seb would be furious and she was unsure that she could cope with any more of his condemnation! Feeling her anguish, Louise put her hand over Kim's and gave it an encouraging squeeze. When Seb jumped nimbly down from the driver's seat and slammed the door, she leaned across and whispered to the frightened girl, "Sure you are not to worry, I will be with you and I prayed an extra rosary for tonight, come on, soon be over."
"That's what I'm afraid of!" Kim muttered to herself grimacing and following Louise out of the vehicle on shaky legs.

Darren bid them goodnight and took off to his home. Seb walked ahead and stood and held the front door open for them.
"Your lover is home!" he hissed as she marched past.
"So I see," she smiled sweetly up into his stern face, trying to stop her thundering heart and the sudden impulse to turn and run. Sensing the panic in her, his fingers curled cruelly around her upper arm and Kim found herself pushed along the hall, there was no escape. Louise stopped to take off her boots, Kim cast her a pleading look but the woman didn't notice.
Seeing her imploring looks at Louise, Seb whispered as he steered her forward, "Don't look so scared sweetheart, I've decided to forget what happened between us this week, your secret's safe with me. I wouldn't dream of giving you away, not because I don't want to, but unlike you I have my brother's feelings at heart!" He lowered his fingers to her elbow and ushered her into the lounge.

12

The room was in darkness except for the flickering light from the fire in the grate, casting a warm rosy glow all around. Alex was sat in a large armchair with Fiona curled up at his feet looking up into his eyes adoringly, while his hand caressed her soft blond curls, both oblivious to the fact that they were no longer alone.

Seb, clearly shaken by the scene before him stopped in his tracks his eyes turning back to Kim, had she imagined the flash of compassion in his eyes? "Very cosy!" he muttered angrily under his breath.

"What's going on Alex?" Seb queried as he switched on the main light, demanding an answer to the obvious intimate scene,

Alex turned towards his brother a little surprised, "Seb, we didn't hear you arrive."

"That's blatantly apparent!"

Alex ignored his brother's remark. "We made excellent time, the roads were clear, and we managed to get on an earlier boat," he stated rising from the chair and helping Fiona to her feet, her eyes fastened on Seb's fearsome appearance, and Fiona looked more than a little scared.

"Are you going to introduce me to the young ...er... lady?" Seb asked sarcastically.

"Seb..." Kim made to explain.

He silenced her, "No, let your lover explain!" Kim felt Seb's hand tighten reassuringly around her arm, 'well what do you know, the man was offering her support!' she thought in amazement resisting the urge to giggle.

"Come in and sit down first," Alex insisted.

"I'm fine standing," he stated, Kim shuddered she could feel the underlying anger in his voice.

"Fine, but it's a long story and I'm sure you'd be better..."

"I'm asking for an explanation!"
Kim quivered at the icy command and thanked God that she wasn't in their shoes.
Alex held his hands up in submission before he dropped his bombshell.
"Ok, but I'd rather you sat down," he paused for breath. "Seb, meet my wife, Fiona."
"Wife! Fiona?" Seb roared looking back at Kim.
"Yes my wife Fiona, we got married in Scotland last Monday!"
"That's illegal, you are already married!" Seb boomed.
"No," Alex shook his blonde head. "The decree absolute came through last week."

For a moment Kim fought with the desire to laugh, but more from nerves than from happiness, then she caught Seb's golden eyes, they seared with savage rage and the desire to laugh instantly faded as she faced his ferocious temper that incredibly was aimed at her, not his brother!
"Explain!" he thundered, "If she's Fiona then who the hell are you?"
Kim winced as he increased the pressure on her arm, and for a moment her throat closed over. She gave a nervous cough and tried to stop the trembling in her voice, "I'm sorry Seb, my name is Kim, Fiona is my twin sister."
There was a deathly silence as Seb digested this information, his eyes narrowed as he spoke, temper was instantly replaced by a sheer look of hurt and disappointment. "I gather that everyone else in the room is in on the joke!" He shook his head as Kim lowered hers.

"Seb don't take it so badly, no-one knew we were eloping, we had to keep it quiet because of Trisha's family," Alex tried to make amends when he witnessed the pain in Kim's face caused by his brother's fury.
"But you told Kim?"
"No...all Kim did was to pretend she was Fiona, we pushed her into it."
"She didn't have to agree to...to...this deceit!" he snarled contemptuously as he let go of her and walked over to the couple.
"Seb that's unfair, what on earth has got into you, if you're going to be cross with anyone it should be me. I'm telling you it wasn't Kim's fault, we asked her, begged her to help us, and in the end tricked her into it," Alex spoke sharply back to his brother. "She probably wouldn't have agreed to help if she had known we were eloping."
Seb ignored his brother's plea of clemency for Kim. "How long have you been planning this, have you given any thought as to how Trisha family will react?"

"It doesn't matter now, we are married, legally, and there is nothing they or anyone else can do about it!" Alex shouted back.
"I thought you had stopped the divorce proceedings!"
"I re-started them last year when I sustained a particularly brutal attack and ended up in a hospital, I just couldn't go on anymore!" He shuddered from the memory and Fiona stroked his arm in comfort, glaring at the irate Seb for daring to attack her husband. Alex took a deep breath and continued his temper under control. "Trisha knew I had re-started them, my solicitors sent her letters, she thought that tearing them up made it null and void!"
"So why didn't you leave the family home again?"
"I didn't need to, at her own request we lived separate lives under the same roof. And anyway I didn't want to arouse her suspicions, I still feared for my safety."
"Okay, but why all the secrecy from your family, couldn't you have trusted me?"
Kim sucked in her breath when she heard the deep ache in his voice.
"Come on Seb, be honest, you sent me to Scotland to separate me from Fiona!"
"I sent you away because I could see the woman you said was your lover ..." he cast Kim a withering look before he continued, "didn't love you!"
"I'm sorry Seb, we were not exactly best buddies, and I know your views on divorce!" Alex was beginning to raise his voice again.
"You know nothing about me or my beliefs," he seethed angrily.

"I think we know enough to appreciate you are behaving very unfairly," Louise entered the room. "Shame on you Seb, you've almost reduced poor Kim to tears, and all she's guilty of is keeping a confidence. One I would have broken long before now to save my own neck! Anyone would think you wished these two lovebirds to be unhappy, don't you think Alex deserves this happiness after all he's been through?"
Seb turned and stared across the room at Louise then shut his eyes for a moment. Kim watched his struggle. He let out a long shuddering breath, "Of course, forgive me, I wish you both every happiness and Louise is right you deserve it, God knows this family has taken enough from you, I'm sorry Alex, Fiona, believe me I'm just a little shocked," he assured them with a sigh. "Welcome to the family Fiona," he spoke holding out his hand towards her.
Fiona was pushed reluctantly forward by Alex, "Thank you Seb, I'm glad to join you," she said raising her cheek for Seb to kiss, with impeccable manners he dutifully obliged. Duties performed Fiona walked over to Kim, "I'm so sorry, am I forgiven for not telling you the truth?" she asked

her sister pleadingly.
"It's not my forgiveness you have to ask for, Mum and Dad will be very disappointed," she answered shakily, breathing deeply to try to regain control of her shattered emotions.
"Don't be cross," Fiona's eyes filled with tears as she hugged Kim.
Kim hugged her sister back, still struggling with her crushed feelings, "I'm not cross, but like Seb I wished you had told us."
"I’m sorry, forgive me?" Fiona stared imploringly into her sister’s eyes.
"I forgive you."
"Right, now everything has been cleared up I think it calls for a celebration, don't you?" Louise asked taking control of the situation. "Where's the champagne Seb?"
"I'll get some." he stated wandering back to where Kim stood.
As he came nearer, Kim felt the adrenaline pump through her veins and resisted the urge to run. Instead she stepped aside while he retrieved the bottle from the drinks cabinet she was standing in front of. He stood up and their eyes clashed, molten golden eyes alive with blazing contempt bit into hers as he spoke softly, "I knew you were lying about something. I should have pushed it further when Paul recognised you, all the clues were there, and your knowledge of animals far outweigh that of an ordinary veterinary nurse. I've been waiting for you to trip yourself up all week. I must say I'm extremely disappointed in you." he uttered cruelly uncaring if the others in the room overheard.
Unshed tears rushed into Kim's eyes as the tension between them reached an unbearable pitch, but she bravely bore his derision.
"I'll get the champagne glasses," Louise said coming to Kim's rescue. "Will you help me Kim?"
Gratefully Kim nodded glad of the chance to get away from the simmering tension in Seb.

Kim sank down gratefully onto the kitchen chair, her legs were trembling so badly that they were no longer supporting her.
"Are you alright?" Louise asked kindly. "I didn't hear what he said to you but I saw the look, and if looks could kill!"
Kim's bottom lip quivered and she shook her head, "No," she whispered as she folded her arms on the table and lowered her head on them. She wanted to give way to the impending tears, but didn't dare, they were going to toast the bride and groom, she still had to go back into the room and face everyone.
"I'll get the glasses, while you sit and get your emotions under control," Louise said patting her shoulders.

Kim sat there while Louise shut the kitchen door, she listened as her friend opened cupboards, and heard the chink of glasses.
"Here drink this! Joan keeps it here for medicinal purposes."
Kim looked up with surprise as a brandy glass filled with amber liquid was pushed into her hand.
"I don't..."
"Drink, sure you don't want that grizzly ol' bear thinking he's got the better of you do you?"
Kim shook her head and managed a weak smile, "No." she answered on a sob.
"Then drink, it'll give you courage!"

Kim downed it in one go, and felt the liquid warm her frozen heart.
"Better?" Louise asked picking up the tray of champagne glasses.
"Um," Kim stated wobbling a little as she stood up. "Oh dear, I think I drank it too fast!"
Louise grinned, she had put more than a double in the glass. "Are you ready to face the monster, now that you have taken the relevant monster repellent?"
"I think so!" she giggled.
"Then what are we waiting for?"
Kim smiled and, opening the door, followed her friend into the lounge feeling a little tipsy but full of Dutch courage, that was strong stuff Louise put in the glass.

"You took your time," Seb stated taking the champagne cork off, and pouring it into the glasses Louise held for him.
"Joan's been rearranging the cupboards, we had to search for the glasses..."
Kim moved into the room putting a safe distance between her and Seb, and sat on the sofa next to her sister.
"Are you alright?" Fiona whispered softly. "What a brute, did he upset you?"
"Nothing I can't handle, Louise gave me a double brandy."
"You don't drink!"
"Louise said it was monster repellent!"
She sucked in her breath as Seb interrupted them and handed both the women a glass of champagne, the look in his glittering golden eyes told her he had overheard her comment.
"To both of you, we all wish you a long and happy life together," Seb said, raising his glass.
"To both of you," Louise and Kim agreed.

Kim stared across at Seb, he was stood one arm leaning on the mantelpiece, as he took a sip of his champagne, laughing down at Louise. His nonchalant air didn't fool her, when their eyes met he made no effort to conceal the smouldering rage and disapproval that he had for her!
Kim lowered her eyes and sipped her champagne, listening to the buzz of conversation going on around her looking for an opportunity to slip out unnoticed. Fiona had moved to Alex's side and the two lovebirds were deep in conversation. Louise was discussing the arrangements for her return to the convent tomorrow morning with Seb, she heard Louise say she was leaving Goldie with Seb for another fortnight, then she was returning to take her back. The effects of the brandy were beginning to wear off and Kim saw her chance of escape. When Seb's back was turned she quietly slipped out of the door making her way to the kitchen for one last look at the puppies, then she would pack her case and hopefully would be gone before anyone was up the next morning. It saddened her that she wouldn't be able to say goodbye to Louise, but they had exchanged addresses, she would write to her.

After packing her case she stood under the shower in her en-suite, letting the needle sharp spray of water ease the tension in her aching body and sober her up a little. 'Damn why did you drink that brandy? You could have been on your way home by now!' she chastised herself. Snapping off the shower she wrapped her warm tingling body up in the fluffy white towelling robe and, swathing her hair up in a towel turban style, walked into the dimly lit bedroom.

Stifling a scream she stared at the overpowering presence of the tall dark figure looking out of her window, half expecting him to evaporate into thin air.
"What the hell are you doing in my room?" she demanded when she managed to find her voice.
He spun around to face her, his eyes burning over her state of undress as he began to walk towards her with a feline stealth.
Nervously she took a few steps back until her back was against the wall, and pulled the top of the robe closer to her neck holding it tight, "Get out!" she commanded, "or I'll call for help."
Seb stopped a few feet in front of her, put his head on one side, his mouth pulled into a derisory smile at her coy action, and folding his arms across the vast breadth of his chest whispered menacingly. "Go ahead Kimberly, scream all you like, Alex and Fiona have opted to stay in the cottage for the weekend seeing that they are still on their honeymoon, and Louise has driven them over there, we're alone for a good hour."

"Why didn't Alex drive himself?" she asked feeling panic rising.
"Louise was the only one of us who wasn't over the limit!"
"It won't take her an hour!"
"She insisted on making up the double bed for them," he drawled stepping nearer.
"I-I warn you, I've taken self defence lessons, just one step nearer and..."
"And what Kimberly, you'll throw me over your shoulder!" he purred with a throaty laugh at the preposterous suggestion, reaching out and touching her cheek gently as if she was a child.
She paled as he stepped even closer, her face was tingling where he'd touched her, "Don't think I wouldn't," she warned bravely, more bravely than she felt.
He nodded and looked down at his feet as he weighed the situation up. "I have no doubt that you would, I can still feel the imprint of your hand on my cheek from the other night," he decided, the twisted smile still on his handsome face. "I had better behave. Besides, you've taken the monster repellent, probably tinged with a clove of garlic, there's no telling what that would do to me!"
"You are not funny Seb, and I don't like your threatening behaviour, you scare me!"
"I'm sorry, I'm not threatening you and I don't mean to scare you, though God knows you should be scared of me after what you've done..."
"Done? All I've done is cover for my sister, if you were more approachable maybe Alex would have confided in you!"
"Thanks, so it's all my fault that my brother ran off like that!"
"If you hadn't sent him away..."
"Oh come on Kim, be fair, seeing you and Alex together that night, I knew you weren't in love. I just wanted to stop Alex from making another mistake. If I'd been more supportive the first time round, if I'd been here, I could have saved him all those years of heartache!"
"Well Alex won't be hurt by Fiona, she loves him and he loves her!"
"I can see that!"
"So why are you here, what do you want?" she asked as she took in his handsome carved features, he was still angry.
"Nothing sinister Kim, so calm down, I'm not about to attack you, contrary to your belief I wouldn't harm a fly! And don't look at me like that!" he pleaded. "I've had an urgent call from the police, a badger has had an altercation with a vehicle, its in urgent need of medication and a place to stay. They are on their way over, I was wandering, seeing that you are obviously a fully qualified vet, if you would assist?"
"Give me five minutes."
"Thanks, I'll be in the kitchen, don’t be too long!" he told her as he

disappeared out of the door, closing it firmly behind him.

13

Dressed in a warm tracksuit, her long wet hair loose over her shoulders, and feeling sober again, Kim marched into the kitchen. "Good evening Miss," the policeman greeted her.
"Good evening," Kim returned, blushing slightly as she recognised the young policeman who had called at the cottage the previous week.
"Sir Worsley tells me you're a vet Ma'am?"
"Yes, where is the patient?"
"In the van, shall I drive over to the 'farm'?" he asked addressing Seb.
"We will see you there," Seb nodded taking hold of Kim's elbow and steering her out of the back door.

Watched by two policemen and Seb, Kim sedated the badger before Seb took the grasper off its neck.
"No broken bones," she stated as her experienced hands felt over the creatures limp body, "An x-ray machine would be useful, there might be internal injuries, though there doesn't appear to be any internal bleeding, his gums are a good colour, let's hope it's only bruising."
Seb nodded in agreement and stated quietly, "I'll get a pen ready for him."
"Right we'll be on our way then, here are the details of where he was found." The young policeman said handing a piece of paper from his notebook over to Seb.

Together they settled the badger in a dark pen, and waited until he started to come round from the anaesthetic before leaving him.
"I'm convinced he's more shocked than anything, I'll check him tomorrow before I..."
"Leave?" Seb finished dryly, locking the door to the hospital and

dropping the keys into his pocket.
"There is no need for me to stay now, the puppies are doing fine."
"And you no longer have to make an idiot of me!" She gasped as his fingers wrapped cruelly around her upper arm and he started to frog march her away from the Manor.
"What are you doing? Let go of me at once," she hollered indignantly trying to struggle free from his vice-like grip, "I'll scream for help!"
"No one will hear you, now stop struggling or I'll physically pick you up and carry you!"
Swallowing down her fear she changed tactics, "Where are you taking me?"
"I want to talk to you, and I don't want to be interrupted, Louise has returned, the car's on the drive."
"Can't it wait, I'm tired and..."
"You'll be gone at daybreak."
"How did you know when...?"
"It's enough that I know."
Kim gulped, then shuddered squashing down the fear that was threatening to overcome her, was he saying he did have the ability to read her mind, or see into the future?

The light from the stable shone through the open door onto the ground, lighting their way across the grass. Seb pushed the door open and gently steered her inside shutting it firmly behind him then folded his arms across his chest, effectively barring any way of escape.
"Well what do you have to say that won't wait?" she whispered licking her suddenly dry lips nervously and tucking a strand of wayward hair behind her ear as she took in the menacing look on his sullen face. So this was showdown time!
Narrowing his golden eyes he took a long shuddering breath, "You owe me an explanation and an apology, I don't take too kindly to being made a fool of!"
"I didn't make a fool of you, at least not deliberately!" she denied.
"Unintentionally or deliberately you still made me look stupid!" he snapped.
"You know I was a victim just as much as you were, I had little choice, I couldn't give them away and I didn't want to cause any more trouble between you and Alex. I'm sorry, now please can I go, I'm tired!"
Kim tried to step past him and squealed. With the stealth of a cat he unfolded his arms and caught hold of her wrists and held them behind her waist, pulling her against his hard body. "You are not leaving yet, I'm not finished!"

"You can't stop me!"
"Oh Kimberly I can," he purred softly
She sucked in her breath, unable to hide the apprehension within her.

A deathly silence descended while he just stared at her, and for a moment Kim thought he was going to kiss her, but abruptly he released her and stepping away, ran a frustrated hand through his jet-black hair. "Don't look at me like that, I won't hurt you, I'm appealing to your better nature. Please stay, at least until Alex and Fiona return to Ashill tomorrow morning."
"Why?"
"Fiona needs to speak to you, she needs to clear up a few things," he said gently holding her arms again.
"She spoke to me earlier!"
"Kim, she didn't get a chance to explain everything, you disappeared, she went to your bedroom but you weren't there!"
"I checked on the puppies before I went upstairs," she stated trying to ignore his hands softly rubbing the tops of her arms, sending all sorts of wild emotions shooting through her body.
"You're trembling are you cold?"
"No, you scared me!"
"I'm sorry you seem to bring out the worst in me. Come!" he said abruptly, leading her over to the straw bales. "Sit down."
Gratefully she sat down, glad to take the strain off her trembling legs, and watched as Seb paced in front of her. "I still don't see why you had to lie to me about your identity?"
"I thought that was obvious, anyway does it matter?"
"It matters to me, you could have let me in on the secret, I feel hurt."
"Look I'm sorry your pride has been hurt but be honest, the first time we met in here, it was you who jumped to the conclusion that I was Fiona," she accused, her anger rising.
"You didn't put me straight, come to think of it, Alex didn't deny it either!" He turned to stare at her, "It wasn't only Fiona, Alex asked you to cover for him too, didn't he?" The look on her face told him his answer. "I should have realised, we were kissing when he came in, his reaction wasn't that of a man passionately in love. I would have killed a man for kissing you...my lover like that!" he corrected.
Kim swallowed and her heartbeat quickened at the very thought of this arrogant man being consumed with jealousy over her!
"I only agreed until they had had the chance to see one another, I wasn't happy...I didn't want to deceive you, but I couldn't break a promise," she whispered lowering her head.

"You could have told me what was going on after they had left, especially when Paul came on the scene, but you just added to the lies."
"I didn't lie to Paul."
"No," he laughed sardonically, his anger returning. "I remember everything you said to him, you were very clever with your answers, you made Paul think you were Fiona too. How did you put it?" he stated sarcastically, "Ah yes, 'I'm sorry, I have a twin, much to my father's consternation, only one of us went to veterinary school and became a vet!' When I questioned you in the pub, again you were economic with the truth. You are obviously well used to telling lies!" he bellowed loudly back making her flinch.
Kim leaped up and shouted back at him, "That's grossly unfair, you don't know me!"
"I wouldn't want to!" he sniped back, his temper flaring.
The big black stallion disturbed by their arguing snorted and pounded the stable floor with his hoof, and gave a loud snort.

Seb muttered under his breath and walked over to the beast, stroking the animal's smooth velvety coat on his neck he whispered reassuringly into its ear.
Kim watched in awe as a strange calm settled over the place.
"What language are you speaking?" Kim asked amazed at the reaction it had over the animal and the atmosphere.
"The language of angels," he smiled coming to stand in front of her again, "now stop changing the subject. So, it wasn't your idea to pretend to be Fiona."
"No."
His long fingers lifted her chin so that she had to look at him, his golden eyes pierced into hers, "You made me think you were an adulteress and a hussy, and for that I apologise, but you didn't defend yourself."
She didn't answer, how could she, wasn't that what she was? This man was a monk, well almost, and she had deliberately tempted him, what he had called her was well deserved.
He watched the emotions cross her beautiful face, "No Kim, you didn't deserve it, you are not a hussy or an adulteress."
Kim sucked in her breath and blushed, the man had done it again, read her thoughts, accurately interpreting how she was feeling! Brushing his hand away she turned her back on him, frightened he may delve too deep and see other emotions that she would rather hide from him. "Can I go now?"
"Will you stay until they come back tomorrow morning?" he whispered.
Kim spun round to face him, hope in her eyes. "Are you asking me?"

His tawny eyes held hers and he laughed a mocking laugh, "Don't flatter yourself sweetheart, it makes no difference to me whether you go or stay. I'm asking you to give Fiona and Alex a chance to make amends?"
"Oh!"
"Besides I promised your sister..."
"Tell them I forgive them."
"Tell them yourself!"
Kim cast him a scornful look, "I'm sure you will do an adequate job! Goodbye Seb."

Seb reached out and caught her arm pulling her against his hard frame, "Just like that?"
Kim's eyes widened like saucers. "What would you suggest Sir, a farewell kiss?" she asked derisively.
A devilish smile tugged at the corners of his mouth as he challenged her, "That sounds more friendly," he purred softly.
Kim's breathing grew shallow, her mouth went dry and her heart beat painfully in her chest causing her body to stir as he bent his head down towards her, she shut her eyes as his lips brushed tantalisingly against hers. She heard his soft groan as he plundered the softness within. Kim pressed her body closer and wrapped her arms around his neck, she moaned as his hands moved from her waist dropping to the swell of her hips and if it were possible he pulled her closer, his lips travelled down her neck and nuzzled in the sensitive hollow.
"Oh Kim what are you doing to me, you're driving me to sin?" he murmured softly against her.
His words were like a splash of cold water on her heated senses and she pushed herself away from him. "I'm not doing anything to you, y-you kissed me!" she said breathlessly gulping in air, trying desperately to calm her beating heart.
His tawny eyes had darkened from the passion he could not hide, "You invited me, maybe I was right about you after all," he stated.
Stung by his cruel words Kim lifted her hand up to his face, but she wasn't quick enough, his strong hand caught her wrist. "Hit me again and I promise you sweetheart, you will live to regret it!"
Kim pulled her hand away from his grasp, stuck out her small chin, "Go to hell!" she snapped.
"I probably will, and take you with me. Now get out of here before I take what you are so freely offering!"

Crushed and hurting Kim rushed blindly out into the cool night, banging the stable door shut after her. She ran to the Manor but paused

as she reached the back door, she could hear Louise singing to herself and the sound of china clinking.
"I can't face anyone!" she muttered quietly to herself. Turning she walked briskly away from the house, all tiredness had left her, maybe a brisk walk would clear her mind.

Kim had no idea how long she had walked, in her hurry to help Seb with the badger she had forgotten to wear her watch, she discovered a small gravel track that led to some wooden steps. Soon she found herself on the private beach, which belonged to the Manor. The sound of the waves lapping on the beach soothed her aching head and calmed her nerves. It was beginning to rain and if she wasn't mistaken that was a rumble of thunder in the distance. "Yes that was definitely a flash," she muttered to herself as she looked out towards the sea. Mounting the beach steps she decided she had better go back before the storm arrived, she looked down ruefully at her tracksuit, it was warm but hardly suitable attire for a downpour! The rain was getting heavier, turning to retrace her steps along the track, a small animal scurried out in front of her darting into the thick undergrowth that edged the uneven path startling her, causing her to lose her footing. She whimpered in pain as her foot twisted and she fell heavily face down on the gravel, hitting her head on a stone.
Splashes of rain stung her injured forehead mingling with the blood and salty tears. With pounding head and aching hands and knees she limped painfully back to the house.

"Damn," she swore softly under her breath, when she tried the back door. Stepping back she looked up at the house, it was in darkness, they had all gone to bed, she was locked out!
Unwilling to knock Seb up she hobbled painfully over to the stable. The last thing she needed was for him to see her in this state, she must look an awful sight! If the stable door was locked she would rather spend the night outside in the rain than ask him for anything!
"Thank God it's open," she mumbled as she let herself into the warm dry stable. Black Fury, Seb's horse snickered. "Sorry to disturb you, but I need to share your room for the night!" she muttered feebly, trying to reassure the animal. Still badly shaken from the fall she lowered her aching body down on the bale of straw she had sat on previously, and taking her handkerchief out of her pocket with shaking hands, she dabbed it on her cut head, "Ouch!" she winced from the pain.
"Well Fury, I can't sit here all night, better make myself a bed and get some sleep," she mumbled to the horse as he turned towards her. "Don't

look like that, I have no intentions of sharing your straw!"
Looking around she noticed Seb's thick woollen riding cape hung up on a hook. "There's my blanket!" she stated standing on tiptoe and pulling it down, sucking in her breath as the material came into contact with her injuries.
Wrapping her handkerchief around a deep graze on her hand, she arranged the straw into a makeshift pillow, then swathed herself up in the thick woollen cloak and lay down foetal position, totally exhausted feeling comforted by the clean smell of Seb on his garment. Despite her shattered emotions and aching body, sleep soon claimed her.

"Kim!"
Kim turned towards the alarmed voice and flinched as the bright florescent light shone into her weary eyes.
"What the hell are you doing here, oh Kim what have you done to yourself?" Seb's tender utterance penetrated her consciousness as he peered over her.
"Ouch!" she moaned as she sat up struggling to untangle herself from the warm cloak. She ached from head to foot. "I tripped over, what time is it?"
A cool hand touched the bump on her head gently, "Two in the morning, is that the only injury you have?" he asked with concern.
Kim shook her head wishing he would go away, she just wanted to curl up and sleep.
"What else have you done?" he demanded as he folded back her covering, "God woman, you're soaking wet!"
"It started to rain!" she told him unnecessarily, "And I've twisted my ankle."
"We need to get you dry, can you walk?"
Too bruised and tired to argue with him Kim nodded, still not fully awake she stood up and with his help she managed to limp over to the door, Seb flicked the light switch off and shut the door behind them.

The rain had stopped, it was a clear night and a full moon shone brightly lighting the path ahead. She took a few steps and the pain in her foot made her cry out.
With a curse Seb bent down and scooped her up into his strong arms.
"Please put me down, I can walk if I can hold onto your arm!"
"I think not, it will take all night, now help me out here and put your arms around my neck!"
Obediently Kim wrapped her arms around his neck, he was wearing a fleecy tracksuit and he felt soft and warm. Unable to resist the sudden

urge she lowered her aching head on his broad shoulder as he carried her silently back to the house, she knew it was her imagination but it felt like he'd leaned his head closer to her and held her tighter. "We'll soon get you comfy," he whispered.

Reaching the back door he lowered her gently down, still supporting her weight while he opened it. Then picking her up again kicked the door shut behind him, "What were you doing in the stable?"
"After I left you I went for a walk along the beach. You locked me out!"
He clicked his tongue, "I thought you were in your room!"
They were at the bottom of the stairs, "I'll walk, I'm far too heavy for you."
"You are not too heavy," he stated taking the stairs with ease.

Pushing her bedroom door open he put her down carefully on the bed and bent down to examine the bump on her head. "Did you knock yourself out?"
"No."
"Have you got blurred vision?"
"She shook her head in the negative, "I saw stars though!" she tried to be humorous.
He didn't laugh but held his hand in front of her. "How many fingers am I holding out?"
"I haven't got concussion if that's what you're asking."
"You were foolish to go to sleep straight after a knock like that, you should have woken me!" he admonished.
"I didn't bang it that hard, my hand hurts more than my head!"
He lifted up her injured hand and gently unwound the blood stained handkerchief and tutted, before examining the other. "They both need cleaning, I can see some gravel in the there. Get those wet things off while I get the first aid box from the kitchen," he ordered releasing her hands. He left the room.

Kim reached under the pillow and pulled out her Victorian night-dress, then looked down at her mud-splattered tracksuit both knees were torn. Her vision blurred as tears gathered in her eyes, with a sob she burst into tears.

"Shall I get Louise to help you?" his voice asked kindly, pushing a big white handkerchief into her hands.
"N-no I don't want anyone to see me like this, I look an absolute mess," she shivered uncontrollably.

He stood staring down at her for a moment then with an expletive he took the night-dress from her. With unsteady hands he pulled her top up, "Come on Kim help me, you're frozen, I don't want you going down with pneumonia!" he spoke abruptly.
Like a small child she raised her hands so that he could slip her top off and drop the white cotton robe over her. She watched his strained face as he pulled in down, covering her nakedness. "Can you lift your bottom?" he asked, before he pulled her trousers off.
"Are you angry with me?" she asked in a small voice, shifting her rear to help his task.
"No I'm not angry with you," he clipped. "Sorry this is going to hurt, you've grazed both knees and the blood has dried." Kim winced a little as he eased the material away from her torn flesh.
"Good girl," he said throwing the trousers down and putting her towelling robe around her shoulders, "I'll clean the wounds up then you can get into bed."

Seb returned from the en-suite with a bowl of disinfectant and opening the first aid box, took out ointment and cotton wool. "I'm afraid this will sting too," he apologised. "Ready?" he enquired his golden eyes holding hers.
She nodded.

Kim stiffened but didn't make a sound as he gently cleaned her injuries of the small stones and blood before he stuck plasters on them. Lifting her injured foot onto his bent knee, he bound it with an elasticated bandage. Lastly he handed her two tablets and a glass of water. "Take these, it'll ease your headache."
"How did you know I was in the stable?" Kim asked handing back the empty glass and wiping her mouth with the back of her least injured hand.
He shrugged his huge shoulders then looked straight into her pain filled eyes. "I just knew something was wrong, that you were in trouble."
"Have you got sixth sense?"
"Probably," he grinned. "Now get into bed child, you're shivering."
Seb removed her robe and held back the sheets while she climbed in then gently tucked her in. "Goodnight Kim," he murmured gently brushing her cheek with his lips.

His gentle compassion overwhelmed her and made her feel vulnerable again but she managed to stop the tears until the light was switched off. When darkness engulfed the room she gave in to heart wrenching sobs, she trembled with emotion and cold.

"Child don't," he pleaded leaning over her.
"I-I thought you had gone, I'm so cold!"
He tutted, and she felt the mattress compress as he sat on the side of the bed, heard the thump as he let his track shoes fall to the floor. Laying down next to her, he drew her up against him, she felt the heat from his protective body even through the duvet, "Better?" he asked huskily snuggling closer to her.

14

Kim awoke to the sound of hushed voices outside the bedroom door. She sat up and looked around the room, her eyes caught sight of the small clock on the table, it was nearly eleven o'clock! Seb had gone but the bed was still warm from where he'd been.

She flushed as the memory of last night flooded back, he had lain on top of the bed for a while, his huge frame wrapped around her keeping her warm. It was early dawn when she remembered him easing himself off the bed.
"Don't go," she begged sleepily.
"I must, for your reputation and my own, if anyone were to find us like this they might misconstrue the situation. Anyway I'm cold..."
Kim held the covers open invitingly, "So am I."
Seb stood very still just looking down at her, in the grey light she could see a myriad of emotions crossing his handsome face as he fought to resist her offer. "You don't know what you're asking, you're temptation with a capital 'T'!" he muttered.
Still she held the covers open invitingly.
For a moment she thought he would go, then with a whispered groan he got into the bed, covering them both with the duvet. He was freezing, that's probably what made her turn and wrap her warm body around him. She frowned, it was her that started the kiss. She remembered he had tried to turn away, tried to protest, his words echoed in her mind causing her heart to leap and beat frantically in her chest.
"Kim, for heavens sake wake up, you don't know what you are doing," he groaned in a dark husky voice. Kim was glad that he thought she was not fully awake, it gave her the excuse to deepen the kiss.
Seb lowered his thick lashes onto his flushed cheeks, and didn't see the

look of triumph in her eyes when with a very masculine growl he submitted and returned kiss for kiss and touch for touch.

"I want you," he trembled with hot passion, turning them both so that he had pinned her gently under his large frame. Mindful of her injuries he supported himself on his elbows, his hands threading into her long silky hair, as golden eyes dark with desire barely visible in the dawn light, pierced hers.

"I can just about stop, is this what you really want?"

"Yes, I want you," she whispered her consent.

"So be it!" he answered as he lowered his dark head, and whispered against her mouth, "I want you too, so badly, but..."

His words were silenced as she shuddered against him, wrapping her arms around his neck and drawing him closer.

For such a large man he was so incredibly gentle, yet so passionate as he carefully disrobed her. "You are beautiful," he groaned as his eyes swept sensually over her before he brushed her parted lips with his.

The moment their mouths met they were lost, any sane thought drowned in a sea of desire that they had both created. She gasped with pleasure as sexy tender kisses traced their way down her throat and further, until they discovered the swell of her breasts, she whimpered in delight as his lips teased the taut nipple, she could hardly bear the exquisite sensations he was causing. "No more," she begged

"You want me to stop?" he growled jubilantly, knowing her answer would be no, he lingered, trifling with her tender flesh until her whole body was burning with hunger for him. She whispered his name in anguish as she threaded her fingers into his thick dark hair, writhing beneath him almost losing control as waves of desire consumed her, his lips left her breasts, finding other sensitive spots before returning his lips to hers in a hot passionate kiss.

Kim's hands gripped his shoulders as she arched herself against him, then getting bolder, temptingly traced her fingers down his masculine curves as he hurriedly undressed, she smiled as the muscles on his superb body rippled beneath her touch. He let out a groan as she explored further. "Darling slow down," he begged, stilling her hand.

"I want you now, Seb," she pleaded, hardly recognising herself, never before had she behaved so wantonly.

He kissed her again as his long legs parted her thighs, but still he held back, allowing his fingers to tease, she cried out his name again as she moved seductively against him, and swallowed a gasp of pain as they became one.

"Sweetheart why didn't you tell me," he groaned as he stroked her face tenderly covering her with kisses. "I've hurt you, shall I stop?"

"Don't you dare," she whispered, pulling his hips closer to her now the pain had subsided.
With great control, still a little nervous of hurting her, he moved slowly inside her. Only relaxing and giving in to passion as she encouraged, bringing them both to an earth shaking climax, she heard him whisper her name as he throbbed powerfully into her, burying his face into her neck. Kim almost cried with the emotion she felt, their bodies had melted into one, their hearts beat in unison, and their spirits had touched. He was her soul mate, they had been one since time began, and would be for eternity, of this she was sure
Contentedly she listened to his laboured breathing and felt his rapid heartbeat against her breast slowing down as he fell into an exhausted sleep. Gently easing herself from under him she snuggled close, "I love you Seb," she whispered before sleep claimed her too.

Seb's irate voice penetrated her thoughts bringing her back from her musings. "For goodness sake Louise, please believe me, it's not what you think..."
"Seb I'm not thinking anything, you don't have to explain, least of all to me. What you do is your own concern, but you've hurt..."
"Don't be angry!" he begged. "I can't believe I allowed this to happen, I shouldn't have. Forgive my weakness."
"I agree you shouldn't have done it, you made a promise to me that..."
"Kim fell over last night she was hurt and shocked, honestly it was her who came on to me..."
"Oh come on Seb. No excuses, you've been trained to resist women! Why don't you face the truth, the sexual tension between the pair of you is obvious. You can't say I didn't warn you, anyway we'll say no more, what's done is done, I only hope it doesn't have any lasting consequences!"
"Lasting consequence?"
"Surely you were taught the facts of life!"
"Oh Heavens I never gave that a thought!"

Kim stifled a hurt cry, Louise must have come in and found them sleeping together, she was obviously hurt and upset, Seb was trying to convince her that it meant nothing to him and that it was all her fault! Another wave of pain shot through her heart as she heard his next words. "I didn't mean for this to happen. I wish to God it hadn't!"
"That hurts Seb!" Kim whispered to herself, then admonished herself. 'What do you expect, he was speaking the truth, it was you who seduced him!' Her face coloured with shame, how could she face him again?

Perhaps she could plead temporary insanity caused from the bump on her head. With another shuddering sigh she threw back the cover and grabbing her discarded night-gown, pulled it quickly over her head covering her nudity. She would have a shower then leave. Seb wouldn't want her here, not after this. Forgetting her twisted ankle she leaped quickly out of bed.
"Ouch!" she grimaced in pain as she fell forward knocking an ornament off the bedside table onto the floor and only just managing to stay upright herself.

"Now what are you doing!" Seb ran into the room followed by a concerned Louise.
"I'm getting up, what does it look like I'm doing?" she winced in pain as she picked up her dressing gown to cover herself.
Louise took one look at her white face, sporting a large mauve and yellow bump on her forehead. "Get back into bed at once! Seb you call the doctor out!" she ordered taking control of the situation.
Kim glanced at Seb's incensed face, he was avoiding eye contact with her, holding his head down. He looked shattered and broken, Kim swallowed, had she reduced him to this? "I don't need a doctor, it's only a sprain, I'm going home today!" she argued watching Seb's face for a reaction, there wasn't one. Well what was she hoping for? For him to beg her not to go, to stay, admit he needed her? The pain around her heart grew worse as the truth descended over her, so he wanted her out!
"It's the lump on your head that is worrying me not your ankle!" Louise spoke firmly.
"Better do as Louise tells you, I wouldn't mess with her!" he answered forlornly still evading eye contact, smoothing his dishevelled hair, he marched out the door.

Kim got back into the bed obediently, too close to tears from the excruciating pain of rejection to argue, she allowed Louise to tuck the covers over her. Seb was so furious with her, the conversation between him and Louise confirmed that, what must he think of her? How degrading, to have a man explaining to his ex girlfriend why he was in another woman's bed! Explaining! Why he was apologising to her! What was even more humiliating, were the words, 'I wish to God it had never happened.' She bit her bottom lip to stop it from trembling, what had she done? This man was going to give his life to God and she had defiled him!
"There now, I'll get you a cup of hot sweet tea and some toast," Louise chatted brightly as she replaced the ornament on the table and picked up

the discarded muddy and torn tracksuit up from the floor where Seb had thrown it last night. "And I'll check that Seb has phoned the doctor."
"I just want to go home," she croaked unable to stop the sob in her throat.
"Shock, that's what it is. Let the tears come, you'll feel much better," Louise sat down on the bed next to her and put a comforting arm around her shoulders as she handed her the tissues.
"I-its not shock, how can you be so kind to me? Don't you realise what we've done, what I've done?" she whispered miserably.
"I can guess and in a way I'm to blame, I was the one to encourage you to start a relationship with him," Louise answered without condemnation.
"Louise I'm so sorry, I didn't mean to deliberately hurt you..."
"Hurt me, what have my feelings got to do with this?"
"I overheard some of your conversation, you sounded very upset, I didn't mean to come between you..."
"The only reason I am upset with Seb is because he took advantage of you. Will you get it into your head once and for all, Seb and I are no longer an item. I've given him a real lecture."
"Seb spoke the truth, it was the exact opposite, I took advantage of him, I seduced him..." Her voice trailed away as she hung her head in remorse and mortification as the tears flowed again.
"I somehow think Seb knew exactly what he was doing, if you seduced him, he allowed you to," she smiled.
"He's so angry with me."
"No, he's not angry with you, he's cross with himself and because I've lectured him about taking advantage of a woman staying under his roof for protection. I also pointed out the risk he has taken, you could be pregnant!"
"He shouldn't concern himself, there is no chance of that. I'm on the pill, a doctor prescribed it for medical reasons," she stated dryly. "So if that's all he's worried about..."
"Now come on, you know him better than that! That is not his main concern, now dry those tears and cheer up. I'll get you some breakfast. Your sister will be over shortly, another reason why you can't leave today, she has lots to share with you, anyway you're in no fit state to travel."

Fiona! Kim had forgotten about her sister, so much had happened since last night. How was she going to explain her awful behaviour, did she need to explain anything to her?
Louise walked in with her breakfast on a tray. "The doctor is calling in on his way home from morning surgery. Your sister is downstairs, she's just arrived with Alex, Seb is filling them in on what happened."
"Oh no," Kim looked horrified.

"Relax, I mean how you came by your injuries," she laughed putting a tray in front of her. "The rest is our secret. Now get some of this down you, you'll feel a lot better."
Kim munched on some toast and jam while Louise chattered excitedly about returning to her work. They both looked up when Seb knocked on the door, "Louise, I need a moment alone with Kim," he requested dejectedly, still avoiding eye contact with Kim.
"Sure," Louise smiled obligingly at them both. "Times getting short, so I'll say my goodbyes now," she leaned over Kim and kissed her. "I'll be in touch, I'd like to take you up on the offer of a weekend at your home in Surrey!"
Kim wanted to beg her to stay, the last thing she needed now was a confrontation with Seb.

The door shut behind Louise, Seb made no attempt to come near her, keeping his distance he stood at the foot of the bed. His face wore a contemptuous mask and she lowered her head when his angry golden eyes clashed with hers, she waited for the onslaught.
"I've come to apologise for last night, it should never have happened."
Kim kept silent, too upset to speak, what to her had been so beautiful, was nothing more than a mistake to him!
"Look at me!" he demanded.
A feeling of sudden shyness overcame Kim and she lowered her head in shame.
"I said look at me!"
When she didn't obey he walked around the bed and his long fingers cupped her chin, giving her no choice but to look into those deep golden eyes. Anger flared up inside her. "If you are concerned about any consequences, as Louise put it so delicately, I can put your mind at rest, I'm on the pill!"
He shut his eyes and sucked his breath in through clenched teeth, "Until Louise said anything it never entered my mind. But I am pleased that it won't cause you further distress."
"Well that's all settled then!" she snapped.
"Have you nothing else to say?"
"There is nothing to say," she answered her eyes brimming and her bottom lip trembling.
"There is, I want your forgiveness for taking advantage of you."
"Why, so that you can go back to your vocation with a clear conscience?"
"My conscience will never be clear of this!"
It was said with such feeling that remorse overtook Kim, she had cost this man a great deal. Freeing herself of his hold she averted her head and

whispered, "It is I who should ask your forgiveness, as you so rightly said, it should never had happened!"
"I'm forgiven?"
She didn't answer.
He sighed. "Kim, I have to go back to Quarr Abbey to..."
"Well where is the patient?"
Kim looked mutely up into Seb's drawn face, he stifled a frustrated curse as the doctor knocked on the door and, interrupting them, walked into the room hindering any further conversation.
"She's here Dr Lucas. Look I'm sorry Kim, I have to go now, I'm dropping Louise off at the ferry terminal, she's going back to her convent..." For once the big man seemed unsure of what to do, then he lowered his head and kissed her chastely on the cheek. "Bye, I'm not sure when..."
"Kim darling, what have you been up..." Fiona waltzed in behind the doctor, stopping as she caught the kiss and the expressions on both their faces. "Oh am I interrupting something?"

Kim swallowed the overwhelming urge to call him back as she watched Seb walk with an air of frustration out of the room. So he was going back to Quarr Abbey, picking up his life at the monastery where he'd left off. Regardless of what had happened between them, she thought, as bitterness welled up within her, and an errant tear flowed down her cheek.
"Hey come on," Fiona admonished as she put her arms round her sister. "Has he been upsetting you again? Cheer up he's leaving in a moment so you don't have to set eyes on him anymore! I've just phoned Mum and Dad they're on their way down here."
The elderly doctor coughed politely, "If I could just examine the patient?"
"Oh I'm sorry of course," Fiona moved away from the bed apologetically.

"Well young lady, you'll live, the ankle is worse than the knock on the head," the doctor stated binding her foot up again. "It's a very bad sprain, I recommend that you keep your weight off it for a week and keep an elasticated bandage on. You were lucky you didn't break it. How did you do it?" he asked.
"I was walking along a path last night and something jumped out and startled me, I think it was a small animal, I turned and twisted my foot!"
"Are you up to date with your tetanus jabs?"
"Yes, I'm a vet!"
"Good, then I'll give you a prescription for some painkillers, take no more than two a day, is that understood?" he ordered peering over his steel

rimmed glasses.
Kim nodded, "Yes. Thank you."
"You're welcome," he replied, doing up his black bag.

Fiona waited until the doctor had left the room. "What were you doing walking along a path at that time of night, you were in bed when I left last night?" Fiona enquired.
"Seb had a call from the police, a badger had been knocked over, he asked me to treat the poor creature."
"But why involve you, he's a qualified vet himself, he studied before going in the monastery he's got a special way with animals!" Fiona informed her.
Kim's mouth fell open in surprise, "He never told me he's a vet!"
"He needed Kim's help to administer the anaesthetics!" Alex barged in adding to the conversation. "I came to tell you he has just left with Louise."

Kim's head was spinning round and round, she needed to be alone. Her heart was aching more than her bodily injuries, Seb had left, and she was never going to see him again! She didn't think she could stand that knowledge. She felt angry and frustrated that they hadn't been given a moment to talk. She wanted to know why he had wittheld the information that he was a qualified vet, and why he'd asked her to help last night when she knew he could have coped on his own. The audacity of the man, he was angry with her for lying to him when he'd done exactly the same to her! Maybe she wasn't entirely to blame for last night after all! He'd deliberately created the situation of them being alone.

It was with relief that Alex and Fiona left her to rest for a while before lunch.
She lay back against the pillows and shut her eyes. 'So Seb must have known all along that she was more than just a vetenary nurse! He must have enjoyed the little game he played. Anger welled up inside her when she thought back over the many different incidents. The first time they had lunch together in the pub and he got her to read the papers, pretending not to understand, then...Ooh...I hate him,' she seethed inwardly.

At twelve o'clock Joan put her head around the door, "Ah you're awake Kim, gosh it's strange to call you that! Master Seb told me that you are Fiona's sister, you where extremely brave to deceive Master Seb like that, was he very angry with you when he found out?"

"At first," Kim grimaced at Joan. "But I suppose I deserved it."
"Well it was only because you were protecting your sister. I can understand why you did it, if Trisha's family had found out they may have tried to stop the wedding..." The woman shuddered, then her face brightened. "Fiona is lovely and they are so in love! Not like his previous marriage," Joan sighed then coloured when she realised she'd said too much.
"Oh, what do you mean?"
"Forget I said anything, I shouldn't have spoken out of turn," she gulped.
"Please tell me, it won't go any further."
Joan sighed, "Well I suppose you'll hear it from others sooner or later. Trisha told Master Alex that she was pregnant. Alex didn't want to marry her but..." she shrugged, "It was a shotgun marriage."
"Trisha's parents?"
"No, Alex's father! Alex was only nineteen, he pleaded his innocence, said he'd never had that sort of a relationship with her, but no one believed him."
"Whose baby was it?"
"There was no baby, she was never pregnant, the woman has never been in her right mind. She told her parents and Alex that she'd miscarried so he stayed with her and tried to make a go of the marriage, besides he had nowhere to go, he couldn't come home, he hated his father for not believing him."
"Poor Alex, didn't Seb believe him?" Kim asked.
"He didn't know anything until after the wedding, he was away at university. Anyway the reason I'm here is Master Alex wants to know if you want to have your lunch downstairs, he'll carry you down if you do!"
"I would like to get up, but I'll get myself downstairs, have you a walking stick?"
"Yes, I'll get your sister to bring it up, she said she'd help you get dressed."

Kim managed to get showered and dressed with a little help from Fiona.
"Tell me more about Seb, he's a very dour man isn't he?" Fiona commented as she pulled a sock over her sister's uninjured foot, watching her sister's face intently.
"He's a little dour yes," Kim agreed.
"You like him though?"
"Of course I like him."
"No really like him!"
"How do you mean?"

"Is there something between you? He looked…well sort of…"
"Don't be ridiculous, anyway as you said earlier, I won't be setting eyes on him ever again!" Kim stated evasively.
"How come you stayed here after I left? Nothing would've persuaded me to stay here alone with the man, why he's very handsome but more than a little scary!" she grimaced.
"Once you get to know him he's okay, anyway we were not alone, his butler lives in the east wing," she replied as nonchalantly as she could, aware when she saw her sister's inquisitive look that Fiona wasn't totally convinced that nothing was going on between her and Seb. Eager to change the subject Kim started questioning her. "Tell me about your week with Alex."

It worked, Fiona was ecstatically happy her whole face shone with a radiance, only too pleased to talk about her beloved husband and their wedding day. "Alex came to the cottage very early the next day. He woke me up but luckily you must have been so tired you didn't hear him. He told me that Seb had caught you in the stables, and that he mistook you for me. That was really handy, because after taking you home, Seb told Alex he was sending him to Scotland on business, that meant I could go with him because Seb didn't know of my existence. I knew you wouldn't give the game away. The awful man sent Alex away to deliberately split us, he told Alex he thought I, well you were only after his inheritance and he could tell I, I mean you, didn't really love Alex! Can you believe that?"
Kim nodded, "He is very astute but he was right, I don't love Alex and he spent the next few days trying to convince me that I didn't!"
"Oh! How did he do that?" she asked frowning enquiringly.
Kim turned away to hide her blush. "By telling me I didn't. I was angry with both of you for putting me in that position!"
"But surely that was your own fault, whatever possessed you to stay here? You should have gone home or stayed at the cottage!" Fiona dismissed her sister's protests.
"The storm had cut the telephone lines, and you had the car keys, Seb was worried about me being alone. Besides Alex had asked him to keep an eye on me, he had a nerve asking Seb to do that," she stated angrily.
"He had to make it look authentic, if he'd gone away and not insisted that his lover wasn't going to be looked after, Seb would have been very suspicious, especially after recent events, Alex was genuinely concerned for your safety. Trisha's family live nearby, if they found out that you were staying in the cottage on your own, there is no telling what they would have done!" she pouted.

Kim sighed, the last thing she needed now was one of Fiona's sulks!
"Of course, I'm sorry, I had decided to go home, Seb was going to take me to the ferry that afternoon."
"Gosh did you sleep all morning then!"
"No," she stated dryly. "Seb had an appointment with someone." Kim frowned as she recalled that meeting. "You really dropped me in it, the man he was meeting was my former university lecturer!"
"Never!" Fiona laughed. "How did you get out of that?"
"I told him I had a twin!"
"And he fell for that, why we aren't a bit alike!"
"Seb wasn't to know that was he? At least it wasn't a lie!"
"True, but it still doesn't explain why you didn't go home that afternoon."
"I wish to God I had," she mumbled under her breath. "Seb's Rottweiler developed a milk infection and it meant he had to bottle feed the litter."
"So?"
"It was such a large litter, and when I saw him filling up a long line of bottles, I took pity on the man and offered to help him!" Kim's face broke into a rueful smile. "You should've seen the mess he was in. There was milk everywhere, he had his best suit on too!"
Fiona giggled, "So you offered to stay and help? You're a sucker for a hard luck story," she admonished.
"Maybe, I couldn't leave him to cope on his own."
"You're so like Dad, which reminds me Mum and Dad will be arriving here sometime after lunch."
"Why?"
"To celebrate my marriage, why else?"
"How did they take it, were they very cross?"
"You know Mum, she was over the moon, Dad was...a little quiet."
'I expect he felt hurt,' Kim kept her remarks to herself. She was glad her father was coming, she needed his big shoulder more than she ever had before.
"Anyway I was telling you about the wedding, we were married by special licence at Gretna Green of all places, it was so romantic," she stated rapturously. "Alex made sure I had the full works, he hired a wonderful wedding dress for me, the photos are being sent here," she mused.
"That's nice," Kim murmured.
"Yes it was, I've married a man in a million! Oh Kim I love him so much!"
"I should hope you do!" Kim answered feeling just a twinge of envy.
Fiona frowned, "You're not still cross with me are you?"
"No, I'm glad it's worked out for you both."

"You look kind of sad!"
"Sad? No, but I'm feeling a little peckish!"
Fiona looked like she might have delved further, then thought better of it, "So am I, Right if you are ready?"
Kim nodded and picking up the walking stick Joan had found for her, limped painfully down the stairs into the large kitchen.

All through the meal Fiona and Alex told Kim and Joan about their wonderful time in Scotland. Kim tried to listen with interest but her mind kept returning to Seb, and the pain in her heart increased as visions of him dressed in priestly gowns flashed before her eyes. "Kim?" Fiona broke into her musings.
"What?" Kim returned looking up from her empty coffee cup.
"You were miles away, are you feeling alright you look terribly upset?"
"I'm fine," she assured Fiona.
"Alex just asked you if you wanted another coffee?"
"Er sorry, no thanks!"
"You look as miserable as my big brother, are you both so opposed to us getting married?" Alex asked, looking a little concerned.
"No, I really am pleased for you both, and I'm more than glad to have a brother like you," she smiled reassuringly at the handsome man.
Alex beamed across the table at Kim. "Thank you, and I am more than pleased to have a sister like you!"
"Of course Kim is pleased, I think she's upset because of something Seb said to her. I interrupted them earlier, I think they were having an argument!" Fiona chipped in, her brown eyes watching Kim's face for clues.
Alex looked compassionately at Kim, "Don't let that old sourpuss upset you, he isn't always..."
"We weren't arguing and he hasn't upset me," she snapped irritably. "Forgive me, I'm sorry, that was uncalled for. My ankle is a little painful."

The doorbell rang stopping any further conversation. 'Saved by the bell!' Kim thought breathing out a sigh of relief.
"It's Mum and Dad," Fiona jumped up, a look of uncertainty crossing her lovely features.
"I'll answer it!" Alex got up before anyone could protest. "Better that I face them first!"
Kim looked across at her twin's apprehensive features. "Stop worrying, everything will be fine!" Kim assured her feeling sorry that she had snapped at her earlier.

"I hope so," Fiona stated grimly.
"Kim's right, they will be over the moon when they see how in love you both are, don't you know the world loves lovers! Now off the two of you go and I'll make a fresh pot of coffee and bring it in into the lounge," Joan stated ordering the two younger women away in the direction that Alex had taken.

A feeling of wretchedness swamped over Kim as she followed Fiona into the lounge to meet their parents, she hung back and watched the two couples before her from the doorway. So wrapped up with Fiona and their new son-in-law her parents hadn't seen her. Her mother's face was shining with delight, she was deep in conversation with Alex and Fiona was hugging the big Irish man, if their father was annoyed with her it was now forgotten judging by the look on his face.
Everyone was so happy, Kim felt the prickle of tears in her eyes and stepped back into the hall, she had to get away.

15

Kim stiffened, her lovely face drained of colour and her breath caught in her throat in a gasp as a large bulk barred her way.

"Going somewhere Kim?" he murmured softly, his lips against her ear.

The walking stick fell from her paralysed fingers to the stone floor with a clatter that echoed around the big hall. She didn't need to turn around, there was only one man whose deep rich voice could make her heart skip, only one man that spoke her name the way he did. His arms had snaked around her waist, if they hadn't she would have fallen.

"I startled you, I'm sorry," he purred in her ear.

She had stepped back straight into Seb. Without turning she whispered, "W-what are you doing here?"

"In case you've forgotten I live here!"

"I know that!" she snapped pulling herself away from him. "You said you were taking Louise to the ferry then..."

"And I've taken Louise to the ferry in Fishbourne, then I went onto Ryde and picked your parents up from the catamaran," he muttered letting his hands fall from her.

"You didn't say you were going to pick them up!" she accused.

"As I remember, we were interrupted!"

"You said you were going back to Quarr..."

"Kim," her father called, "No hug for your old father?"

Seb picked the walking stick up off the floor and handed it to her, his golden eyes penetrating into hers. "Your father's speaking to you. We will get a chance to speak later."

With the help of Seb's hand on her arm and the other in the small of

her back, without another word, she was pushed forward into the room. Kim limped painfully into her father's embrace.
"What have you been doing to yourself?" her father groaned as his kind face took in her injuries.
"I'm fine, just been a little clumsy," she explained watching Seb as he walked past them towards his brother.
"I think another champagne is in order, Joan's bringing the glasses through," Seb informed the party.
Her father looked at Seb then back to Kim's strained white face and took her aside. "You don't look fine and I'm not just referring to your physical wounds." With that she was hugged against him. "What's really wrong?" her father whispered softly, so no one else heard.
"I want to go home," she whispered back, her bottom lip began to tremble.
"Because of Seb?"
Kim didn't answer.
The big man sighed and led her into the hall, "I've an important conference to attend in London on Tuesday so I'm returning to the mainland tomorrow, but your mother is staying on until next weekend, at Seb's invitation. I'll join her again on Saturday, is tomorrow soon enough?"
"Tomorrows fine, Fiona's car is outside."
"Good, I'll phone for a ferry booking, then we'll leave sometime after lunch."
"Thank you."
Her father nodded and squeezed his daughter's arm supportively, holding her a little away from him so he could see her face. "Come on, chin up, we are supposed to be celebrating your sister's marriage!"
"Hey, father of the bride, we are waiting for you to propose a toast to the happy couple!" her mother's voice interrupted them.
"Coming," her father answered, "Are you ready?"
Kim smiled back and nodded, finding strength in her father's love as he led her to join the others in the celebration.

The wedding breakfast was served buffet style in a spectacular banqueting hall on the first floor of the building, its huge patio doors at one end overlooked the grounds and beyond, giving a magnificent view of the English Channel. Feeling in need of a breath of fresh air, Kim sipped her champagne and nibbled on a sandwich as she hobbled over to

one of the open doors and stepped carefully out onto an ornate balcony. Away from the other guests, she enjoyed the cool evening breeze, as it wafted over her hot face as she stood by the iron railings, looking down she sucked in her breath, when she realised she was standing above the patio where she had met her former university lecturer. Because of her elevated position she had a wonderful view of the landscaped garden as it dropped away towards the sea. Flights of shallow steps, decorated with Italian statues and flowering pots descended to the private beach below, the one she must have walked on last night. So engrossed with the beauty before her she jumped and almost spilt her champagne.
"Admiring the beauty?"
She turned and watched Seb sauntering over to her, his tawny eyes skimming over her in a look as blatantly physical as a caress.
"You have a wonderful home, I didn't realise this balcony was here!"
"If you had you would have realised I watched you on the first day you came," Seb told her unabashed.
"W-why?" she asked glancing up into his brilliant golden eyes.
"I was trying to work out who you were, why you were here. I thought if I could just see you, observe you, the answer would come!"
"And did it?" she asked desperately conscious of his nearness.
"Does it matter, I know now!" he raised his glass to drain the contents.
"I don't like the idea that I was being watched..."
"There was nothing sinister about it, I just didn't trust you, I knew you were hiding something from me..." he stopped talking as Kim's father walked through the window and joined them. Kim muttered an excuse and left the two men.

The evening went well, after that brief encounter, her father kept Seb deep in conversation and when Seb had taken her father to see the puppies Kim said her good nights, using her ankle as reason to retire early. Painfully she managed to undress and shower on her own. Climbing wearily into bed her mind flew to Seb. Why was he back here? This morning he had told her he was returning to Quarr Abbey. 'Don't even think about him!' her mind admonished her as even thinking of him made her body ache with a craving that ran far deeper than desire for him. Sighing, she picked up her book, but her mind wouldn't focus on the riveting story before her, she had read and reread the same page three times. In frustration she threw it down on the bedside table and was just about to switch the bedside lamp off when there was a knock on the door,

it was probably her father.
"Come in," she called sitting herself up and patting the top sheet into order.

The door opened and she watched in horror as Seb entered and shut the door behind him. He moved with feline grace over to the chair by the side of her bed. "May I?" he asked before lowering his very physical male frame onto the soft feminine cushion and crossing his legs. Kim could do nothing but stare, she tried to tell him to go but no sound came from her open mouth. His stunning magnetism made her heart race and her body shudder with anticipation. If he demanded that he have her now she knew she would be unable to resist him.
"It seems fate is always keeping us apart but we still need to talk," he informed her.
Kim cleared her throat, "Say what you have to say then go," she managed in a squeaky voice.
Flashing her a scathing glance his face darkened with anger as he drew his brows together in a scowl, making him look very demonic. She shuddered again but more through fear than desire this time as his golden eyes bore into hers. "Very well," he thundered, "I came here to apologise again for what happened last night. Louise was right, I took advantage of the situation. I accept full responsibility, you are in no way to blame, you were still in shock from your accident and not thinking straight. We...there is a chemistry between us, it would be foolish for either of us to deny, but nevertheless my action was still inexcusable. I'm asking you again, I need your forgiveness."
"Just like that?"
"Woman what more do you want?"
His words rung around the room, and she lowered her head letting her long lashes drop onto her cheeks shielding her sudden bewilderment from him as she studied the backs of her hands.
"Ah I get it!" he exclaimed aggressively, pushing the chair back and leaning over her, his hands either side of her pinning her down.
Kim looked up into his tawny eyes confusion on her beautiful face, every breath she breathed seemed insufficient. "What?"
"You're looking at your bare fingers and wondering what a gold band would look like and you'll settle for nothing less!"
"No!" she denied hotly.
"No? In the monastery we were warned of women like you and Trisha,

hell bent on seduction. Maybe I shouldn't have listened to Louise, I think you planned the whole thing. The perfect opportunity came your way, but unluckily for you, I am not Alex, I would never fall for that trick!"
The little colour that was in her face drained away, and pure rage came to her rescue overriding the excruciating pain around her broken heart, "How dare you? Get out!" she whispered holding his gaze. "Just get out!"
Seb contemptuous eyes pierced angrily into hers as he banged both his fists hard against the covers making the bed shake, before he pushed himself upright and left the room.

Kim starred at the wooden door, he hadn't slammed it, but the noise of it closing jarred her heart. With a shuddering sob she turned her head into the pillow and wept. He thought she had seduced him so she could trick him into marriage, just like Trisha had tricked Alex.

Kim lay on her back staring at the ceiling, the grandfather clock in the hall chimed yet another hour. "Three o'clock," she told her brain that was in overdrive, frantically going over and over the argument with Seb. Sighing she threw back the rumpled covers and picked up her robe, perhaps a cup of tea might help to induce sleep.

The house was silent, so she carefully descended the stairs clinging tightly to the banister rail, wincing with pain as her ankle protested. Luckily the kitchen was well lit by the outside security light so she was able to find everything she needed without switching a light on.
Tears streamed down her face and her lip trembled as she sat at the kitchen table and drank her tea, sobs still raking her small shoulders. The puppies in the next room must have heard her, they were beginning to whimper and Susie was beginning to whine. If she didn't quieten them down they would have the whole household awake.
Rinsing her cup under the tap and tying the cord from her gown tighter she opened the room where the dogs were.
"Sshh!" she whispered as Louise's dog Goldie padded over to her. "It's only me, go back to your bed."
The dog licked her hand and obediently went back to settle down next to Tiny Tim.
"Good girl," she murmured as she sat down on the camp bed that she had slept on when they had fed the puppies. She shivered and took the

blanket that was folded neatly beside her and pulled it around her, tears fell as she remembered pulling Seb's cloak around her yesterday. Yesterday? Was it only yesterday he had carried her back to the house cleaned her wounds and...fresh tears fell, and completely devastated, she lay down curling her aching body up into a protective ball sobbing helplessly.

* * *

Seb dismounted gracefully from his horse and led the elegant beast back into the stable, frowning he shrugged out of his riding cloak and hung it back on the hook. His long fingers lingered on the robe that had enveloped her. He had taken Black Fury for a ride in the early hours of the morning to try to erase the images of Kim out of his mind. It hadn't worked, the very robe he had around him smelt of her perfume, reminding him of the events of last night again and again as Black Fury galloped over the downs. Never before had he been able to experience another person's emotions. Why he had actually touched her soul, their spirits had entwined, they had become one in every sense of the word, and probably would be for all eternity and it scared him, because she was nothing more than a conniving little...! If he didn't know any better he could well take in the belief she was Lady Rose reincarnated! Pushing the irrational thought away, he sighed deeply as he unsaddled his horse and after brushing him down and throwing a blanket over him, gave him fresh hay. He patted the stallion's neck lovingly and spoke to him before he closed the gate to his pen, and walking over to the door switched the light out.

Letting himself into the kitchen he walked over to the cupboard where Joan kept her 'medicinal purposes only' brandy, and poured himself a large drink, he was in need of some medication! Picking up the glass he took a swig and wandered over to the room where the puppies were. The door was open and he frowned, he couldn't have shut it after he'd shown Kim's father the litter!

The room was dark and if she hadn't sobbed in her sleep he wouldn't have realised she was there. She was lying on the camp bed curled up in a ball, her even breathing interrupted every now and again by a shuddering sob that shook her small frame.

It hurt, the sound of her tormented sleep cut deep into his very heart! Despite her failed plan, he had still been the one who had caused her pain and it distressed him more than anything ever had before! Why he allowed himself to feel her grief he didn't understand, she had brought it on herself. From the outset she had tried to seduce him. Finishing the rest of his brandy in one gulp, he put the glass down on a side table and sat down gently next to her, his healing hand automatically reached out and gently rubbed her back as he prayed over her. He nearly groaned aloud as he felt her pain more intensely. Soon the sobs ebbed away and she drifted into a peaceful sleep. As his eyes adjusted to the dark he could see her beautiful face, it was nearly his undoing, he had to get away. Groaning softly he lifted his hand gently off her, and his eyes caught his mother's Celtic ring that he wore on his little finger. Without really thinking he took it off and reaching for her tiny left hand, slid it onto her third finger. It came as no surprise that it fit perfectly, some still small voice deep inside told him it belonged to her now, and he was in no mood to argue. Besides arguing with that precious voice was never a good idea. The moment he sealed the action with a kiss to her hand he felt the cover of a blessing surrounding them both, it spoke of forgiveness and unconditional love, perhaps now there would be an end to these feelings he was experiencing. Getting up he picked up another blanket and wrapped it around her then left the room, he had an early start tomorrow. 'Tomorrow,' he questioned himself as he looked at the clock on the kitchen wall, it wasn't even worth going to bed!

Goldie's wet licks on her cold bare feet woke her, and for a moment she didn't know where she was. Then memories flooded painfully back, with a groan she pushed the blanket aside and sitting up stretched her weary body. The hall clock chimed she counted six, "Sorry Goldie, it's not time for breakfast yet," she said stroking the soft golden fur as she stood up. Folding the blankets, she put them back where she had found them and made her way back to her bedroom, it wouldn't do for anyone to find her there, least of all Seb!

Shutting her bedroom door she walked over to the window and drew the curtains, the sun was just rising and was throwing a wonderful warm peachy glow all around, casting long shadows on the front drive. It promised to be another beautiful warm day. She pressed her forehead against the cold glass in an effort to follow the antics of a small bird, she

laughed and wiped away the mist her breath had made on the window, it was then that a tall dark figure caught her eye. She sucked in her breath, it was Seb. He had his back towards her and he was putting a case into his car boot. Tears welled up in her eyes as she took in his dark attire, he was dressed in a monk's habit. "No!" she whispered in a strangled cry. "Please don't go back, don't you know you belong to me, you always have and you always will!" It was as if he heard her heart's cry, at that moment he turned and looked straight up at her window, if she didn't know any better she could have sworn their eyes had met. Surely he couldn't see her, he was too far away! Carefully she shrank back from the window into the room, her heart beat painfully in her chest when she heard the car boot slam and the engine fire, she moved towards the window again and watched tearfully as the vehicle disappeared down the drive until it went out of sight.
She let out a strangled cry of pain, and crumpled down onto the floor. He was gone, the only man she had ever loved. She didn't cry anymore there were no more tears, she was totally cried out.

Without thinking she quickly showered and dressed in a pair of white cotton drill trousers and a navy striped 'T' shirt, applying plenty of make-up to try and conceal the tell tale signs of excessive weeping. It was as she was combing her hair in front of the dressing table mirror that she noticed the golden Celtic ring on her third finger of her left hand as a ray of sunlight caught it. The hairbrush she was holding fell onto the carpeted floor and she held her hand disbelievingly in front of her. The ring Seb wore on the little finger of his left hand was adorning her hand! Her heart thumped painfully in her chest and her legs felt like jelly. She lowered herself down on the dressing table stool.
"I don't understand," she whispered to herself as she twisted the gold ring round her finger. How on earth had it got there? Seb was wearing it last night, she'd noticed it when he'd sat down on the chair next to her bed. She shut her eyes and realisation hit her as the dream she had last night drifted back into her mind, she had dreamt that Seb had been with her in the puppies room. He had spoken to her in his strange language, and stroked her back soothingly. An eerie feeling made her shiver as she remembered his hands holding hers and slipping the ring onto her finger, then his lips kissing the ring. "Spooky!" she muttered to herself. Then sanity took over, it couldn't have been a dream, Seb must have been there in the flesh, and given her his ring. Confusion swept over her, but why

had he done that? He was going back to the priesthood today, why should he give her his ring! A dry sob escaped, it was almost as if he was leaving it in payment of what she'd given him, ease his guilt! "I hate you," she whispered, wishing she could tell him to his face. Her conscience told her to take the wretched thing off but her heart wanted to keep it there because she felt closer to him. Her heart won, somehow it would be wrong to take it off. Putting a dress ring on the same finger to hide it she squared her shoulders, stuck out her small pointed chin and walked down to the kitchen still using the walking stick.

"Good morning Kim, help yourself to cereal," Joan called over her shoulder as she cracked an egg into the frying pan, "Toast is on it's way."
"Good morning Joan, thanks, morning Dad," she said bending down and kissing her father's cheek.
Her father frowned at the dark smudges under his daughter's puffy eyes, but knew better than to comment. "We're leaving earlier than planned I could only get booked on the eleven o'clock ferry, is that alright with you?"
"Thanks," she whispered sending him an appreciative smile as she sat down next to him.
"Bad night?"
"Ankle played up," she lied.
"Oh, so it was you that had a cup of tea in the middle of the night?" Joan asked leaning her ample body over the table to put the toast in the rack.
"Yes," Kim answered puzzled.
"I saw the mug on the draining board," she explained. "You didn't have a brandy too?"
"Good grief no!"
"Must have been Master Seb, the bottle was on the worktop and I found the glass in the puppies room, Darren said he was riding his horse in the middle of the night! The world's gone mad!" she tutted going back to the cooker.
Kim blushed and busied herself with buttering her toast. So the great man, like her, had been unable to sleep, well, she was glad! And it confirmed that he had been with her last night.
"Are you packed?" her father asked. "I thought we'd leave around ten, we have to be there half an hour before it sails."
"I can be ready by then. I did most of my packing last night."

16

Seb turned his car and drove through the narrow entrance to the tree lined drive of the medieval Quarr Abbey. At the end of the drive his wheels crunched to a stop outside the double wooden doors in the bay marked 'residents only'. With a heavy aching heart he opened the boot of his car and withdrew his case, he had seen her, felt her heart cry out in pain as he drove away. It felt like he'd been hit with a brick in his chest and it took all his strength not to turn around and go back to her. But he couldn't, he knew that to cancel today would be wrong.
"Brother Seb!"
He looked around to see the elderly Brother Joseph dressed in his black robes hurrying arthritically over to him. Seb smiled a smile that failed to reach his eyes and locked his car, then ambled towards his friend and confessor.
"Good to see you again Brother Seb I missed you, we were so sorry to hear about the death of your dear father," he said crossing himself reverently. "We lift you and your family up in prayer at Mass everyday."
"Thank you Brother Joseph," he said greeting the old fellow with a hug.
"You have things to tell me, I can see it in your face, we will have some time together before the service. But for the moment the Archbishop is here, he's going to take the ceremony so you're very honoured," Brother Joseph informed Seb as they walked into the building. "Brother Robert is waiting for you in his office, he wanted to see you before you got changed in your room, leave your case there I'll get Brother Dominic to carry it up to your room for you."

Seb knocked on the Abbott's door and waited for the command to

enter.
"Come."
The Abbott looked up and smiled, "Welcome Brother Sebastian, sit down you look weary."
"I didn't sleep too well last night."
"Too excited or are you having second thoughts, it's a mighty thing you are undertaking?"
Seb shook his head, "No I've never been more sure, it's what I know the Lord has called me to do."
"Well the Archbishop has honoured us with his presence, and he will take the service."
"So Brother Joseph tells me, I am indeed honoured," Seb smiled.
"Not only that the other news I have for you is that your 'parish' is ready and waiting," he chuckled. "The only snag is we haven't found a housekeeper yet. But Mrs Clark, she's been a parishioner for sixty years, is going to cook an evening meal for you until you can find someone."
"Thank you, I appreciate what you've all done for me."
"It has been a pleasure for all of us to help you find your true vocation in life. Now you have one hour before the ceremony begins, Brother Joseph will be assisting you with your robes."
"Robes?" Seb asked.
"We knew you wouldn't have thought of them so Brother Jonathan specially tailored them, it is his special gift to you."

Seb looked at his image in the mirror, his white embroidered robe made him smile.
"Do you like it?" Brother Joseph laughed.
Seb grinned, "I do, it's very apt."
"Tailor made, I'd say. Well that's the bell are we ready?"
Seb took a deep breath, he wished his family could be here to witness this, but most of all he wished Kim was by his side, maybe she would then understand why he had to go through with it. 'What was he thinking?' he pulled himself up and took a deep breath. "I'm ready, and thank you Brother for your wisdom."
Brother Joseph smiled and patted Seb's arm,"You are doing the right thing, all will come right with time."

* * *

"...Go forth to love and serve the Lord. May he bless you in your

chosen vocation, may you be a good shepherd to your flock, in the name of the Father and the Son and the Holy Spirit, and the people said..."
"Amen!" the chorus of voices agreed.
Seb rose from his prostrated position at the altar steps, turned and faced the congregation and smiled when he saw Louise. At least he hadn't been totally alone, he appreciated her presence, she'd said yesterday she hoped to get to the ceremony. The organ struck up and he grinned at the choice of hymn.
"Brother Paul chose that for you!" Brother Joseph whispered with a smile as he took his place behind Seb.
Seb nodded his approval as he walked behind the procession of holy men out of the chapel to the tune of 'All Things Bright and Beautiful'.

"I'm glad you made it," Seb walked across to Louise and kissed her cheek, are you going now?"
"Yes I managed to get a lift from the Bishop's secretary, he's returning to Portsmouth now."
"I didn't think they would allow you another day."
"I had marked this in the calendar weeks ago, they didn't mind."
"Well I'm grateful, I needed..."
"You didn't ask your family?"
"No!"
"You haven't told them have you?"
"No, I didn't really have a chance did I, can we change the subject?"
"If you want, when do you start your new position?"
"Officially in a fortnight's time, but I'm going there tonight. I need time to think and repent."
Louise nodded, "I dig your robe."
"It was part of their present to me," Seb smiled.
"Based on St Francis of Assisi I take it?"
Seb's smile broke into a broad grin as he held the robe up to take a closer look at the exquisite embroidery that the nuns of St Cecelia's had sewn. "The animals gave that away!"
"Look Seb, it's none of my business but..."
"You're right, it's none of your business."
"Okay," Louise grimaced and held her hands up in surrender. "I must go, Father John is waiting for me and I've got to prepare for my class tomorrow."
"Forgive me, I've hurt you," he muttered holding his head down in shame.

"I'm going back to the Manor next weekend, I'll tell them all then, Alex will make a good job of running Ashill and the horses, he's talking of turning it back to a stud farm."
"And Kim?" she dared to ask.
"She's not there."
"How do you know?"
"I know," he muttered forlornly feeling the pain of separation. "But I'll promise you this, I will be seeing her soon. Perhaps you will say a prayer for us."
"That I can promise, now I really must go," she smiled reaching up on tiptoe to kiss his cheek.

* * *

Patrick Brennan was loading his daughter's cases into the car when Fiona and Alex arrived from the cottage. Fiona sauntered over to her father.
"You're not leaving now?"
"Afraid so my dear," he stated closing the boot.
"Why the rush Dad? I thought you were going this afternoon!"
"Urgent case I'm afraid and the only booking I could get was the eleven o'clock ferry, I'm coming back on Friday instead of Saturday so don't have a go at me!" he pleaded.
"Kim's going with you?"
"I've asked her to help me," he explained.
"I thought we were going to be together for a whole week," Fiona stated sulkily.
"Well I would have thought you would want to be alone, this is your honeymoon after all!"
"That was last week," she complained. "First Seb, then you and Kim."
Her father smiled. "Perhaps you could help your mother rustle us up a coffee before we set off?"

After checking in case she'd forgotten anything, Kim stood and looked with sadness around the elegant room. With a sigh she shut the door taking all the memories with her and moved slowly down the stairs, Joan had rebound her ankle and it seemed a lot better, although still very stiff.
"Just got up?" her sister asked as she walked into the kitchen.

"Cheek, I've been up since seven!"
"You look as if you've been up all night, your eyes look awfully swollen," her mother commented, concern on her lovely face.
"Her ankle was playing her up during the night," her father explained for her.
"Oh I'm sorry, well sit down and drink your coffee. I think you ought to go and see Dr Hogan, book an appointment as soon as you get home," she said fussing around her and pushing her gently down onto a chair.
Kim took the cup from her and sipped at the hot steamy liquid gratefully. She needed caffeine and lots of it!
"New ring?" Fiona stopped her chatter mid sentence to look at her sister's hand.
"Had it ages," Kim answered putting her left hand in her lap.
"Let's see."
Kim slipped the dress ring off under the table and handed it to her sister to see with her right hand. "I bought it from the new jewellers that opened in the high street."
"Very nice," Fiona said handing it back, "but I was talking about the other one."
Kim looked to her father as she took the dress ring from her. "Time to go I'm afraid." Patrick stood up looking pointedly at his watch.
"Oh Dad, can't you leave later?" Fiona grumbled.
"No, you know the situation with that stretch of water," he smiled patting his daughter's face, "Are you ready Kim?"
"I am," she smiled gratefully at him, giving her mother a hug and a kiss, then her sister.
"Thanks for all your help, I really appreciate what you did for us," Alex said giving her a hug too. "Remember you are more than welcome to come here anytime you want."
"Thank you, I will."

* * *

"Thank you dear," Patrick Brennan smiled as his daughter put a coffee cup down on the small table. "Now for goodness sake, come and sit down and tell me what's troubling you. You haven't sat still since we got in, surely there is nothing more to do?"
Kim sat down in the armchair opposite her father and waited until he'd filled and lit his pipe. "I don't know how to tell you, I'm afraid you might

be very ashamed of me," she stated softly her lovely blue eyes filling with tears again.

"I doubt that, I might be old but I'm quite unshockable you know," he grinned taking a few puffs. "My experience over the years is that a problem shared is a problem halved. Why don't you start from the beginning."

"I'm in love with Seb."

"I know that, I take it you think he doesn't feel the same way about you?"

"I don't think Dad, I know! He hates me, when he first met me he thought I was only after Alex's money."

"Oh, what made him think that?"

"Right from the beginning he saw the worst in me. He mistook me for Fiona and told me I wasn't in love with Alex."

"Well he was right, you weren't!"

"But Fiona was, is!" she corrected. "Then when w-we kissed he thought I was double crossing Alex."

"If you both kissed then surely he was double crossing his brother too!"

"No!" she denied, "It was me who seduced him!"

"Is that so?" Patrick Brennan asked with a twinkle in his blue eyes. "Well he was correct when he said you were not in love with Alex, you can't blame him for being astute, whose idea was it that you pretended to be Fiona?"

"I'm not sure really, Seb assumed, Alex took advantage and I agreed to carry on the pretence until Alex could speak to Fiona!"

"And Fiona tricked you into carrying on the pretence so they could get married?"

"Yes."

"Personally I think you should have told Seb the next morning."

"I couldn't, Fiona..."

"Fiona...Kim you are always covering for Fiona!"

"Seb was very...he made me angry, with his bombastic ways, Alex is a grown man, he shouldn't be controlling his life. He's been through a very hard time with his first wife!"

"But that was Alex's problem, not yours to sort out for him!" he replied crossly. "Anyway, Seb knows you were a victim too. He can't blame you now!" he continued.

"Yes he can, on top of that he thinks I'm also a liar!"

"You told him lies?"

"Of course I did, by pretending to be Fiona."

"But he knows why now. Didn't Fiona tell him that she left you little choice in the deception?"
"Yes and Alex did!"
"Well there you are then!"
"It gets worse. Dad I seduced him, I lured him into my bed and w-we made love..." she lowered her head afraid to see the condemnation in her father's face.
There was silence for a moment, just the sound of the lighter flicking into action as he ignited the sweet smelling tobacco, while the wise man chose his words. He puffed some smoke into the air, "And the man hated it I suppose, fought you all the way?"
"Dad, he's a priest."
"No he isn't, well not yet anyway, and if he's any sense he'll never be one. It's obvious that the law of celibacy is not one he can adhere to! Now tell me why are you wearing his ring?"
Kim looked down at the band of gold and twisted it nervously around, "I don't know. Last night we had an almighty row, he thought I'd lured him into bed to trick him into marriage, the same way that Trisha had tricked Alex."
Her father swore under his breath, "He said that, he likened you to that woman?"
Kim nodded, "He misconstrued my action...I was looking down at my hands when he was shouting at me asking me what I wanted from him. He thought I was wondering what his ring would look like on my finger...he also said he was warned about women like me!"
"Was he indeed? So he gave you his ring anyway and you accepted it!" he father rasped angrily, and giving up on trying to light his pipe, put it down on the hearth with a bang. "Girlie where's your pride, have you none?"
"No I didn't accept it, I don't understand." She got up from her chair and walked around the room tears filling her eyes at her father's harsh accusation. "Last night I couldn't sleep so I went downstairs and made myself a cup of tea. The puppies were stirring so I went into them to settle them down, I was afraid they would waken the whole household. I fell asleep on the camp bed! The ring was on my finger the next morning. Joan said Seb had left a brandy glass in the room. He must have put it on my finger while I was sleeping."
Her father re-lit the pipe and drew on it thoughtfully, falling silent for a while. "Did you know the ring was very special to him. It was his

mother's wedding ring?"
"No," she denied amazed that Seb should have given her something from his mother. She remembered his disgust when he found out Alex had given the woman's bracelet to his mistress, what had he said? "My mother wouldn't have approved!" Now here she was, his lover, his seducer, wearing his mother's wedding ring!
"How do you know it was his mother's wedding ring?"
"He told your mother, she was admiring it, it's pretty unusual!"
Kim twisted it around her finger, "It's Celtic, would you mind awfully if I went to bed, I feel really tired?"
He got up from his chair and walked over to her, putting an arm around her dejected form. "No girlie, I expect you're shattered, try to get some sleep," he advised, bending down to kiss her salty cheeks. "And just remember I love you very much, and I don't condemn you."

Her father was returning to the Island the following Friday. "Sure you won't come back with me?" her father asked. "I hate the thought of you being alone all weekend. From what I understand Seb won't be there, you might enjoy it!"
"Thanks but no, I won't be totally on my own, I phoned Mandy and, now my foot is better, we are going shopping tomorrow. Honestly Dad, I'll be fine."
"Sure?"
"Go," she laughed pushing him playfully into his car. "Give my love to everyone."
"I will, and mind you don't encourage your boss's wife to spend all his hard earned money!"
"Would I do that to my boss?" she laughed as he drove away. The laughter died on her lips as she walked back to the empty house, it was going to be a long lonely weekend.

As things turned out, her boss called her on the Sunday Morning. "Kim, Mandy said you were on you own this weekend, can I ask you to assist with an emergency Caesar?"
"Sure, I'll be glad to."
"Thanks, Mrs Jolliffe's Yorkshire Terrier has gone into labour and an X-ray has revealed the puppies are very large, and there are six!"
"Goodness, I'm on my way!"

"That was sad," Kim said removing her surgical gloves.
"Yes but at least four survived and mum's doing well, the father must have been a Great Dane!"
Kim giggled at the picture it provoked.
"Thought that would bring a smile to your face!" her boss grinned. "Are you coming back for a bite to eat, Mandy said I was to bring you, she's a little worried about you and I must admit you look awfully tired?"
"Thanks but Mum and Dad come back early this evening and I've promised them a meal would be waiting."
"Ok, I'll get Mandy to phone and arrange another time, I better phone Mrs Jolliffe and tell her she's a grandmother to four Great Dane's," he grimaced.
Kim grinned, "I think you're exaggerating a little, they're not that big!"
"Maybe not, but they are not far off, well off you go, don't come in until later tomorrow, give my regards to your parents."

Kim arrived at the surgery at nine the following day, despite what her boss John Staten had said she would rather be working, it stopped her mind from thinking of Seb. Besides, Monday mornings were their busiest times and it would be unfair to load more work onto her colleagues.

In fact the day was particularly busy. Spring came with it's many casualties. Although they were a town practice, they were situated on the outskirts and were linked to several farms. Three lambs were in the waiting room along with dogs and cats. The RSPCA had bought in several injured birds, so by six o'clock Kim was ready for home. She was just finishing her paperwork when reception rang through.
"Kim we have a patient wanting to see someone urgently, can you deal with it?"
"Yes send them through," she put the receiver down and sighed. "Why do people do that, they know our hours of the surgery!" Kim muttered under her breath.

"Come in!" she invited when the client knocked on her door, she continued to work on some paperwork. Her back turned towards the door, without looking up she spoke, "Sorry I'll be with you in a moment, put the animal on the table."
Kim finished her report and, putting the pen in her top pocket, turned

around. The colour drained from her face, her legs turned to jelly and her heart rate tripled, for a moment she thought she was going to faint and grabbed hold of the desk behind her for support. "Seb?"

Dressed in a grey mac over a dark suit, he stood there with Tiny Tim in his arms, he was so handsome her heart did a double flip.
"I-is he ill?" she asked finding her strength returning, she walked towards the examining table her legs unsteady but determined not to let him see her distress. Why had he brought the dog here for treatment? Her mind was going round and round. Oh yes she remembered, her father had said some of the puppies were going to homes in this area, but he was a qualified vet himself. Perhaps he needed a second opinion.
Seb put Tiny down on the table and nodded, "He's very sick," he confirmed his tawny piecing eyes never left her face.
"Can't you treat him yourself, after all from what people have told me you are more qualified than I?" she retorted sarcastically.
"I'm too close to the patient," he informed her brushing off her sarcasm.
Kim sighed and picked up her stethoscope.
"What are the symptoms?"
Seb's deep husky voice echoed around the small room. "Heart keeps beating erratically."
"Is he experiencing any pain?
"Yes, he can't sleep because of it."
"Any loss of appetite?"
"Yes."
"Weight loss?"
"Yes."
Kim frowned, the puppy looked extremely healthy, his coat shone and his nose was wet.
"He looks alright, hold him for me while I listen to his heart."
Kim watched as his long fingers held the pup with such gentleness, it reminded her of when they'd made love and she trembled. He was so big, yet so mild, he was a gentle giant!
Pulling herself together she put all her effort into concentrating on her patient, putting the ear-pieces into her ears she positioned the stethoscope over the pups heart, she smiled as the small creature licked her fingers.
"There is nothing wrong with his heart. In fact his heart sounds very strong!" she frowned as she raised her eyes to meet his.
"No you are wrong," he stated seductively, taking her hand that was

holding the end of stethoscope from the animal's chest. Kim watched in amazement as he pushed his mac and jacket aside and put it over his own chest. All she was aware of was the heat from his hand and the healthy pounding of his heart filling her ears. Like a zombie she held it over his heart unable to move, his eyes were laughing, but his face was serious as he leaned closer across the table, his eyes still piecing into hers, he held the ear-pieces away from her ears, "I was referring to my heart."
"Oh!" she answered, thinking any minute now she would wake up.
Seb let go of the ear-pieces and leant over the table, his hands gently holding her face, she shut her eyes when his lips touched hers in a gentle seductive kiss which sent his heart rate beating a tad too fast in her ears. Kim came to her senses and pulled her hand away, took off the stethoscope and brushed her heavy hair away from her flushed face. "Look Seb, why are you here, I don't think you are being funny?"
He straightened and put his head on one side. "I'm not trying to be funny, Tiny misses you," he told her softly.
"Oh and what about you?"
"I'm here aren't I?"
"Yes but why?"
"I miss you."
"Why? You hate me, you think I'm a hussy, adulteress, liar, gold digger and a seducer.
Seb groaned, "Did I call you all those names?"
"Yes, and more," she answered. "So why don't you just tell me why you are here then go!"
"I'm here because I'm head over heals in love with you."
"Priesthood didn't work out for you?" she asked sarcastically.
"If I hadn't left the monastic life two years ago, I would have been thrown out, they knew I was unsuitable."
"But you said you were going back!"
"I never told you that!"
Kim chewed her bottom lip and averted her gaze, no he had never said that, but he'd led her to believe it! "You let me to think you were going back to the priesthood!"
"When?" he spread his hands out before her.
"You said you had to go back to Quarr Abbey, you said that the day you took Louise to the boat," she accused.
"Yes but…"
"No," she threw her hands up into the air. "I don't want to hear anymore

of your excuses, I'm sorry that the priesthood didn't work out for you, but you can't just waltz in here and expect me to stand in its place."

"Please hear me out..."

"No, I don't want to listen. Please leave Seb!"

Kim turned her back on him, and closed her eyes when she heard him put Tiny back into his carrier, when the door shut quietly behind him she stiffened. 'No more tears!' she chided herself as she tidied up the papers before her. She jumped when the phone rang. "Yes?"

"Kim, the man with the puppy, he's taken off his mac and he's climbed up on...oh no...oh Lord he's jumped..."

"Call an ambulance!" she cried slamming the phone down.

17

Kim ran blindly across the road towards the bridge through the busy evening traffic, ignoring the irate blasts from the horns, her heart pounding in her temples, dreading what she would see she peered over the edge.
"Seb!" she screamed.

"Get help, I can't hang on much longer!" Seb pleaded breathlessly.
The receptionist ran up to her. "An ambulance is on its way and someone has just phoned the fire brigade..."
"Hold on darling, helps on its way. I love you...Oh God, please hold on." Kim sobbed back.

Seb breathed a sigh of relief when he heard the welcome sound of the sirens. Her words of love and encouragement were giving new strength to his stiff fingers as he gripped the young boy's coat. It was with relief as a fireman took his burden from him. "Be back for you in two minutes, can you hold on Sir?"
Seb nodded, he could do all things now he knew Kim loved him.

Kim climbed into the ambulance with Seb and wrapping a blanket around his shaking shoulders kissed his cold cheek, then sat down next to him and held his frozen hand.
"What happened?" Kim asked.
"I wasn't going to start a row in your surgery, so I decided to sit on the bench by the river and wait until you came out. I wasn't going to give you up that easy. As I got nearer I heard the boy shouting for help, when I looked over the bridge he was in the water holding onto a branch, he

was losing his grip, the current was pretty strong. So I jumped in after him, I was able to hold onto the metal of the bridge and I just caught his jacket as he let go."
"Thank God you're both alright!" she whispered her prayer.
"So you don't hate me that much?" he whispered.
"I don't hate you, I never have."
"Then maybe in time..."
"Seb I couldn't live without you, I love you so much."
He groaned, "Your timings perfect, you tell me something like that when I can't even kiss you!"
"Why not?" she giggled leaning closer to him.
"Why not?" he agreed as his lips met hers.
The young boy was just coming round. "I want my mummy," he whimpered.
"What's you name?" the paramedic questioned him.
"Joe."
"Joe, where does Mummy live?"

After the doctor gave Seb a shot of antibiotics, Kim phoned for a taxi to take them home. Joe's mother arrived to thank them just before they left the hospital.
"I've told him time and time again about fishing in that river! I'm sorry he's caused you both such a fright. And your suit! It's ruined!"
"Think nothing of it, it's replaceable, your son isn't, I'm glad I heard him shouting," Seb assured the woman as he looked down at his wet clothing.
"Better get you home before you catch a cold!" Kim said taking his arm.
"What happened to Tiny?" Seb suddenly looked alarmed, he'd forgotten all about the animal.
"My receptionist is taking him to my home."

Seb wandered into the kitchen, he had showered and was wearing some of her father's clothes. Kim pushed a mug of hot soup into his hand. Her mother laughed at the jeans that were sat precariously on his slim hips, "I'll get you a belt!" she stated leaving them on their own.
Seb watched her go then put the mug down and scooped Kim into his arms.
"I love you," he stated softly just holding her close.
"I love you, I nearly lost you!" she trembled.
"No you didn't, we will be together for eternity."
"I couldn't exist without you."
"You will never have to, can we talk. We need to get a few things straight?"

"Go in the lounge, I'll see you are not disturbed," her mother smiled as she returned, holding out a belt to Seb.

He kissed her breathless after she shut the lounge door, then sat her down on the settee and knelt before her.
"Aren't you going to hold your cross up at me?" she asked with a teasing smile on her face as she wrapped her arms lovingly around his neck.
"My cross?"
"When we kissed once you held your crucifix up to me as if I were an evil to be rid of!"
"When?" he queried with a frown on his face as he tried to recall such an incident.
"I-In the stable you held the cross around your neck and told me you couldn't kiss me because of your vow, you were so contemptuous!"
"I held it tight," he stated with a smile as he remembered. "So tight that it was digging into my hand, by concentrating on the pain and praying for God's mercy I could hold onto my senses and resist you. At that time I really thought I was in love with my brother's lover and I vowed I would never let him down again. The contempt that showed on my face was not all for you, I was angry with myself."
"I was equally angry with myself too, you were almost a priest and there I was leading you to sin!"
"I wasn't almost a priest, anyway that would have been a whole lot easier. I was fighting my feelings for you for one reason alone and that was the fact that you belonged…or I thought you belonged to Alex."
"And I thought you hated me because I was threatening your priesthood!"
"Kim, I have never hated you, I tried to hate you, but everything about you was so sweet and loving. Your behaviour contradicted what I thought you were, every time I saw you, I loved you more and more." He stopped to kiss her before he went on. "At first I was under the impression that you knew the whole story of my encounter with the priesthood, then when I realised you didn't, I admit I used it to my advantage to keep you at a distance. The only reason I went back to Quarr that day was because they have funded my vocation and arranged the ceremony to bless the new venture."
"You said you wanted to follow your vocation and leave the Manor to Alex."
"I still do."
"I don't understand?"
My vocation, my new venture, is not the small place on the Manor but an animal rescue centre with the facility to operate on horses. I now run a hospital for injured wild animals. I went to university to become a vet,

when the Brothers realised I wasn't cut out for the priesthood, they built the hospital and a house for me. It has been their project for the last three years, their way of helping the local Island community."
Kim whispered, "You deliberately led me to believe that you were entering the priesthood!
His arms snaked tenderly around her waist, she felt so weary that she didn't have the strength to resist, her head fell against his big chest. "Forgive me, I honestly didn't mean to hurt you, I was in an awful position, I was falling in love with my brother's lover. I had to push you away, so I led you to believe I was taking Holy Orders," he whispered as he soothed her hair.
"You were not the only one, Fiona and Louise told me you were in the monastery and that you left to help your father when he became ill, but once you knew I wasn't Fiona you could have told me the truth," she sniffed.
"I was very angry with you for lying to me, I couldn't think straight and I'm afraid the sin of pride got the better of me," he stated remorsefully. "And as for me leaving the monastery to look after a sick father, that was only the half of it, the week before Dad took ill I was told very kindly that I hadn't got the calling!"
"D-did that upset you?" she asked wiping her tears away.
"No, I wasn't much good at this celibacy thing," he grimaced and actually blushed.
She giggled, "I did wonder, you didn't make love to me like a bumbling virgin!"
A guttural laugh bubbled in his throat. "I hope not. I've been a fool, I haven't handled things very well, have I?"
"No, you were very unkind to me that evening before you left! Did you really think I was like Trisha?"
"No," he whispered pulling her closer, "But I was very unsure of your motives. You played the part of Fiona extremely well, and I wasn't sure that you were still not playing a role. Your deception cut deep, I'd convinced myself that if you felt anything for me, you would have told me the truth at the start."
"I wanted to, on several occasions I nearly did, I hated myself."
"Well don't, I realise now that I'd allowed my fears to cloud my vision. My love for you is so intense it scared me, I feel everything you feel, I know when you hurt. I'm used to the spiritual things but this is so fierce. We're heart to heart," he stated kissing the top of her head, "I resented the power you wield over me, I'd seen what that power can do to a man. Trisha wielded it over Alex and my family, in the end it almost destroyed my brother and his life. So I tried to make you keep your distance, push

you away by my anger, can you find it in your heart to forgive me?"
"Maybe," she teased. "What about Louise?"
"What about Louise?"
"She was very hurt the morning she found us together!"
"She was, but she was hurt for you. You were supposed to be under my care and I'd taken advantage of you!"
"That's not true, Seb, I seduced you, the things you called me were true, I deserved your contempt."
"No you didn't deserve my contempt, I seduced you. If it had been anyone else I would have woken Louise to assist me. I didn't want that, I wanted you to myself. I stupidly thought that if I let our desire run its course it would then fade and die and leave me in peace again."
"And did it?"
"Oh sweetheart, it just got worse, when I left that morning I felt like my heart had been ripped from my chest, it hurt so bad!"
"But you still left!"
"I had to, I couldn't let the monks down, they have been working so hard towards this venture, and I was still reeling from shock at the intensity of our love!"
"And what about Louise? You said you'd taken a vow!"
"I was young and stupid and my pride was hurt. But it was no vow, a vow is two sided, a covenant between two people. I made the vow with myself. Louise never entered the pact with me! I love Louise, but as a sister only and I found that out after being in Quarr for six months. I had time to think things through, I discovered the only thing that hurt was my self-esteem. But you my love, my soul mate, I love you forever."
His golden eyes pierced into hers, "Good job I'm kneeling, will you enter into a vow with me?"
"What sort of vow?"
"Will you marry me?"
"Yes," she answered tears of joy trickling down her lovely face. "I love you so much."
"Thank you," he answered reaching out and catching her left hand he tried to remove his mother's wedding ring.
"Don't," she pleaded.
His eyes pieced into hers and he smiled as he kissed her hand and slipped a diamond solitaire on her finger over the wedding ring. "You will want a wedding ring of your own at our wedding?"
"No, if I may I want this one."
"I was hoping you would say that, I knew I had judged your motives wrongly the moment I slipped it on your finger, I felt His love binding us together and blessing us, in His eyes we are already married."

"I feel it too, that's why I don't want to take it off!"
"I believe that we've been one for always."
"Do you think we have...I mean, the legend, Lady Rose..."
He laughed, "I must admit the thought did cross my mind, the night of the storm when the tree was struck, for a moment the light must have played tricks on my eyes. I thought I saw a figure of a woman, it evaporated," he shrugged, "it must have been smoke!"
Kim shuddered, "Spooky."
"Hmm, to top that, I have a portrait of her in the library, you certainly have a passing resemblance to her...it made me trace the records back to see what had really happened!"
"Did you find out?"
"I did, apparently she gave birth to ten children and died an old lady. The legend arose because one of my ancestors was into smuggling. He hid the contraband in the cottage and spread the story around to keep people away."
"Was she happy?"
"Not as happy as I am," he drew her closer.

It was Tiny's whimpering that ended the kiss, which was fast getting out of hand.
Kim gently pushed Seb aside, stood up and went over to the little dog, and sat down. "Oh Tiny!" Kim spoke softly to the small abandoned creature sat forlornly in a dog basket by the fire, "Are we ignoring you?"
"Perhaps I should whimper!" he teased, following her he sank down onto his knees next to her and wrapped his strong arms around her waist and nuzzled the sensitive part of her neck. "I've decided to keep Tiny, I want you to have him."
"Oh Seb thank you."
"Will you come back to the Island with me now?"
"I don't know if John..."
"I took the liberty of asking if your boss would release you..."
"You did, when?"
"Before I came to see you, we are good friends we go back a long time."
"I didn't know. What did he say?"
"After he tore me off a strip for making you so miserable he gave me his blessing, as long as you were in agreement!" he stated an anxious look crossed his face as he waited for her answer.
"I'm in agreement."
Seb sighed with relief, "I want you to see your new home."
"New home?"
"The brothers have built a cottage next to the hospital."

"What will happen to Ashill Manor?"
"I offered it to Alex, he refused. He said he's had more than his fair share of Dad's money, but he will live there for the time being with Fiona and run a stud farm, he's building a family home nearby."
"What about Trisha and her family, won't they cause trouble for them?"
"No, they have finally admitted their daughter needs help, she's receiving that at the private clinic. Her father is selling his business and when Trisha is better the whole family are emigrating to America. Her father's family are American, and they have a thriving business over there. He told me his brother has offered him the post of company director."
"I'm glad, I hope she makes a speedy recovery," she said compassionately.
"Yes so do I! Anyway back to more cheerful things, Alex's home will be finished late next year!"
"You want to go back to Ashill Manor when their home is built?"
"Would you mind?"
"Seb I'd love to, it's a beautiful place. But its not the place, I would live in a shed as long as you are there."
"Well for the time being I don't think you'll be disappointed with the cottage the monks have built for us, but as I said, it won't be big enough to raise a family."
"How big a family do you think we will have?" she asked with a look of trepidation.
"Two, three?"
"Four?"
"Four is good," he smiled his eyes filling with love for her. "Can I ask you another favour?"
"Yes."
"Will you help me run the animal hospital? Until our children arrive that is?"
"Thought you would never ask."
"You have made me the happiest man alive, I better speak to your father, I have to ask him for your hand. I want the wedding ceremony to be very soon. Brother Joseph gave me such a penance when I confessed what I'd done, it will take me months to say it!"
"In that case we better make it as soon as possible!" she laughed giving him another kiss.